WITHDRAWN

CHERRY AMES AT HILTON HOSPITAL

CHERRY AMES NURSE STORIES

CHERRY AMES AT HILTON HOSPITAL

By

HELEN WELLS

SPRINGER PUBLISHING COMPANY

New York

Springer Publishing Company, LLC
11 West 42nd Street
New York, NY 10036-8002
www.springerpub.com

Acquisitions Editor: Sally J. Barhydt
Series Editor: Harriet S. Forman
Production Editor: Carol Cain
Cover design: Mimi Flow
Composition: Apex Publishing, LLC

15 16 17 18 / 5 4

Library of Congress Cataloging-in-Publication Data

Wells, Helen, 1910-
    Cherry Ames at Hilton Hospital / by Helen Wells.
        p. cm. — (Cherry Ames nurse stories)
    Summary: Cherry learns about the workings of the mind as she collaborates with a staff psychiatrist in trying to assist a young amnesia patient regain his memory.
    ISBN-13: 978-0-8261-0421-2 (alk. paper)
    ISBN-10: 0-8261-0421-5 (alk. paper)
    [1. Nurses—Fiction. 2. Amnesia—Fiction. 3. Psychiatry—Fiction.]   I. Title.

PZ7.W4644Cbj 2007
[Fic]—dc22

                                                                  2007024056

Printed in the United States of America by Maple Press

Contents

~~~~~~

Foreword

Helen Wells, the author of the Cherry Ames stories, said, "I've always thought of nursing, and perhaps you have, too, as just about the most exciting, important, and rewarding profession there is. Can you think of any other skill that is *always* needed by everybody, everywhere?"

I was and still am a fan of Cherry Ames. Her courageous dedication to her patients; her exciting escapades; her thirst for knowledge; her intelligent application of her nursing skills; and the respect she achieved as a registered nurse (RN) all made it clear to me that I was going to follow in her footsteps and become a nurse—nothing else would do.

Thousands of other young readers were motivated by Cherry Ames to become RNs as well. Through her thought-provoking stories, Cherry Ames led a steady stream of students into schools of nursing across the country well into the 1960s and 1970s when the series ended.

Readers who remember enjoying these books in the past will take pleasure in reading them again now—whether or not they chose nursing as their life's work. Perhaps they will share them with others and even motivate a person or two to choose nursing as their career.

My nursing path has been rich and satisfying. I have delivered babies, cared for people in hospitals and in their homes, and saved lives. I have worked at the bedside and served as an administrator, I have published journals, written articles, taught students, consulted, and given expert testimony. Never once did I regret my decision to become a nurse.

During the time I was publishing a nursing journal, I became acquainted with Robert Wells, brother of Helen Wells. In the course of conversation I learned that Ms. Wells had passed on and left the Cherry Ames copyright to Mr. Wells. Because there is a shortage of nurses here in the US today, I thought, "Why not bring Cherry back to motivate a whole new generation of young people? Why not ask Mr. Wells for the copyright to Cherry Ames?" Mr. Wells agreed, and the republished series is dedicated both to Helen Wells, the original author, and to her brother, Robert Wells, who transferred the rights to me. I am proud to ensure the continuation of Cherry Ames into the twenty-first century.

The final dedication is to you, both new and former readers of Cherry Ames: It is my dream that you enjoy

Cherry's nursing skills as well as her escapades. I hope that young readers will feel motivated to choose nursing as their life's work. Remember, as Helen Wells herself said: there's no other skill that's *"always* needed by everybody, everywhere."

Harriet Schulman Forman, RN, EdD
Series Editor

CHERRY AMES AT HILTON HOSPITAL

CHAPTER I

Identity Unknown

CHERRY AND HER FELLOW NURSE ON THE MEN'S ORTHO-
pedic Ward, Ruth Dale, were preparing a dozen breakfast trays in the small ward kitchen. They moved as
quickly as they could, white uniforms rustling, as they
dished out hot cereal from the food cart from the main
kitchen, and poured glasses of orange juice and milk.

"Faster!" Ruth Dale said. "Last July we had hopes of
getting extra nurses, and here it is September tenth,
and the hospital is still short of nurses."

"Unless you count me as extra," Cherry said.

She was taking the place of a staff nurse who had
gone abroad for a long-planned vacation. On Cherry's
return home to Hilton, Illinois, a week ago, after her
summer job as camp nurse, the post at Hilton Hospital was open. When the hospital asked her to fill in,
Cherry had jumped at this chance to return to staff
nursing.

"It keeps you alert," she thought. "Keeps you up to date on new methods." It was stimulating to work every day from seven A.M. to three P.M. with other nurses and the resident and visiting physicians—to talk with other white-uniformed staff from the Medical Ward, Children's Pavilion, the Operating Rooms. . . . "Why, I never realized how much I missed working in a hospital. I'll *have* to come back regularly and be one of the team."

Mrs. Peters, head nurse for Men's Orthopedics, looked in. She asked brusquely if they'd seen the night nurse's report book and whether the diet kitchen had sent up Mr. Pape's special foods. If Millie Peters sounded a little peppery, it was out of concern for the patients. The two nurses knew that and moved faster.

"I wonder what sort of a shorthanded day we'll have," Ruth said.

"You never know," Cherry commented as she picked up a breakfast tray. "You just never know what's going to happen in a hospital."

She darted out to the ward, smiling her very prettiest for the men in beds, casts, and wheelchairs. The sixteen-year-old boy in the wheelchair, Tommy, was undergoing a course of corrective surgery. The young man in the end bed was suffering from inflammation of the joints and could not move. The big man who had developed osteomyelitis following an auto accident—the old man with a broken hip—the long-term spine patient—all had a long fight to get well. Cherry had told her family she wished she could wear a red ribbon in her hair, or have more music on the ward, to brighten up these patients.

In spite of their serious handicaps, this was a cheerful ward. The men joked about "the peculiar shape we're in," and smiled back at Cherry as she served the breakfast trays. Some of them had said they felt better just having her around. "You're so darn healthy, and you're nice to look at, too, Miss Cherry." She was tall and slim, with cherry-red cheeks and dark curls and a spirited way of moving.

After breakfast she gave her assigned patients their morning care, then wrote up each man's chart for the medical doctors' and surgeons' visits.

At midmorning Dr. Ray Watson came in. He was in charge of Men's Orthopedics, and he reminded Cherry of a clumsy, warmhearted grandfather bear.

"Very good," he boomed as he examined Tommy. "Very nice improvement." He went down the row of beds, accompanied by the nurses, checking the patients and noisily encouraging each one.

The head nurse glanced at Cherry and her look said: "I'm afraid Dr. Watson is a little rambunctious for some of the sicker ones, but his heart is in the right place."

When he had completed his rounds, he conferred privately with the three nurses at Mrs. Peters' desk and wrote out orders for continuing care.

"It's a lot for the three of you to handle," Dr. Watson said. "If only we had more nurses! Glad Miss Ames is filling in here. Well, if you should want me, I'm going to look in at Emergency now."

Dr. Watson thumped away, and the ward settled down for a rest before lunchtime.

About twenty minutes later Cherry was surprised when Mrs. Peters summoned her to the ward telephone. The head nurse seemed surprised, too.

"Miss Ames, Dr. Watson wants you to come down to Emergency and help him with an accident case that's just been brought in. A fracture, but apparently something special. He'd rather have a nurse from Orthopedics than one of the Emergency nurses—for follow-up, I gather—anyway, the nurses are all busy down there. I guess he thinks of you as our 'extra' nurse. Can you safely leave the ward?"

"Yes, Mrs. Peters. I'm all finished with morning routine, if you can spare me for serving lunch."

"I'll get a volunteer to do that." The head nurse spoke into the phone: "All right, Dr. Watson, I'll send Miss Ames down to you." The head nurse listened for a moment. "Yes, Doctor, if you feel privacy is advisable, we'll get the side room ready." She hung up.

"The side room?" Cherry asked as she started for the corridor and elevator. "What sort of case is it?"

"I don't know. Dr. Watson sounded rather uncertain himself."

In Emergency on the street floor, Cherry passed an ambulance attendant wheeling in a badly burned woman and caught a glimpse of doctors and nurses administering oxygen to two workmen in overalls. Cherry found

Dr. Ray Watson in one of the partitioned-off cubicles. A nurse had already set up a treatment tray in there for him.

In the cubicle, on one of the high iron beds, was a dazed-looking young man. His leg was broken and in a splint, but what impressed Cherry was his blank, lost expression. She noticed his ragged but clean clothing. What had happened to him?

"Ah, Miss Ames!" Dr. Watson looked anxious. "Glad you're here. I've examined his leg, and given a sedative, but between you and me—" The elderly doctor drew her aside, out of the patient's hearing. "This boy's fracture is the least of his troubles. He won't talk to me or the orderly or the ambulance attendant who brought him in. He's not in shock, either. No mouth or throat injury. Not deaf. No concussion. He just won't talk to anybody. Maybe a girl would be gentler with him. See if you can get him to speak."

"Yes, Doctor. Perhaps he's too frightened to speak. How did the accident happen?"

"A motorist found him out on Lincoln Highway, lying beside the highway with a broken leg. He called the police, they called our ambulance, and our man put a splint on the leg and brought him in. We don't know whether a car struck him, or he fell from a car or truck, or what."

Dr. Watson told Cherry that an X ray of the patient's leg had already been taken. It was a simple fracture of the lower leg, the tibia, and Dr. Watson had pretty well decided how to set the fractured bone.

"His leg is scraped and dirty. Clean it up and dress it, Miss Ames. You'd better remove his shoes and socks while you're at it."

"Yes, Doctor." Cherry turned toward the dazed man.

"Now see if you can get him to talk to you," Dr. Watson said. "Maybe I'm too gruff. I'll be just outside the doorway."

Cherry approached the young man. He looked straight at her but apparently did not see her. His eyes seemed to be full of tears or glazed, and he lay on the bed stiff as a wooden puppet. Cherry said in a low voice:

"Hello. I'm your nurse."

This time his eyes focused and he saw her. But he might as well have been staring at a ghost.

"We're going to take good care of you here," Cherry said. "You're in a hospital now."

He closed his eyes for an instant. Was it an answer? Cherry felt something sad, tense, and remote in this young man. He was gaunt and wind-burned; about twenty-five years old. Not a tramp; the face was that of an intelligent if distressed man. Cherry bent over him and whispered:

"Are you in pain?" He seemed to be.

No answer. In back of them, Cherry heard Dr. Watson's heavy breathing. She wiped the leg clean with sterile gauze and covered it lightly with a sterile dressing. She noticed the young man's broken shoes; they must be uncomfortable. Removing them and the worn, clean socks, Cherry found that his feet were blistered.

"You must have walked a long way. Your feet look awfully sore."

Cherry gestured to Dr. Watson to come look at the blistered feet. The orthopedic specialist stepped into the cubicle, looked, and shook his head.

"Bathe his feet with a warm, weak sterile saline solution, then with green soap and water."

Cherry made the solution and in silence gently bathed the patient's feet. She glanced up to find that Dr. Watson had left them alone, and the patient was looking at her gratefully. She smiled at him.

"Won't you tell me your name?"

His lips formed the words and then the sound came out with difficulty. "I think it's Bob Smith."

I think—! Cherry was careful not to show her shock. She told him her own name, and said this was Hilton Hospital. They conversed in whispers.

"Are you from Hilton, or around here?"

"No."

"Where are you from? The Admitting Office will want to know."

"I don't know."

"Never mind. You'll remember later."

"I can't remember anything. I don't know who I am, or where I came from, or where I work, not even what my work is—" He struggled to sit up, in panic.

"It's all right. Rest, now." Cherry eased him back against the pillow. She heard Dr. Watson's voice outside the room. "The doctor will help you. And I'll stay with you, if you want me."

"Yes."

Cherry signaled and Dr. Watson entered. Cherry murmured one word: "Amnesia." It meant loss of memory, and was as real an illness as the man's broken leg. The doctor gave her a quick look, nodded, and began to examine the patient's general physical condition. Cherry stayed, ready to assist the doctor. She smiled encouragingly at their patient.

The young man did not speak when they questioned him, and they did not press him. When the examination was over, Dr. Watson called Cherry out of the room.

"Nurse, I want you to stay with this young fellow while we set his leg. You're the only one he'll talk to, so far. We'll set it right away, because he's in pain—there's no swelling, so no need to wait. We'll probably be able to get Dr. Hope over here by tomorrow."

"Dr. Hope, sir?"

"We haven't any Psychiatric Pavilion here, but I'm sure Harry Hope will come over. A young man and a good doctor. He used to be a resident medical doctor here at Hilton Hospital, got interested in—fascinated, I should say—in curing people's minds and emotions as well as their bodies. They're all linked together, you know. He left us to train further."

Dr. Hope was now a junior psychiatrist on the staff of the University College of Medicine, not many miles away. He and his young family still lived in Hilton.

"He'll come over. If Hope says it's necessary, we'll move this boy to a special hospital. But with that leg and low vitality of his, I'd rather not move him at all. Hey, Miss Ames, you don't feel any qualms about a loss-of-memory patient, do you?"

"No, Doctor. I just hope I'll be a skillful enough nurse for him."

"Good girl. Looks like a nice young fellow, doesn't he? Now you see why I wanted that quiet room off your ward for him."

Cherry took a minute to telephone her ward and ask Mrs. Peters to get an orthopedic bed ready. This bed had boards under the mattress, and hand straps for the patient to pull himself up to a sitting position. Then Cherry and an orderly took Bob Smith on a wheeled stretcher upstairs to the side room. There the orderly undressed him and put a hospital gown on him. Cherry went along with the patient to the Cast Room.

Dr. Watson gave a local anesthetic: he injected Novocain into the fracture area. Then, with great care, he reduced the fracture; that is, he placed the two ends of the broken bone together, under the skin. Bob Smith was nervous. He kept looking at Cherry, who wiped his forehead and murmured encouragement.

"There, young fellow, we're all done!" Dr. Watson said. "You're lucky this is a simple break, without swelling. No traction for you! We'll put this leg of yours in a lightweight cast, so you can be up on crutches before you know it."

The young man broke into a sweat. Dr. Watson was too hearty, too noisy; Cherry dropped her own voice to a whisper. A plaster of Paris cast was put on the patient's leg. His badly blistered foot was not enclosed in the cast, but left exposed so Cherry could treat it to prevent infection. Then another X ray was taken to make sure that the alignment of the bones had not been disturbed when the cast was applied.

Cherry accompanied Bob Smith while an orderly wheeled him back to the private room just off Men's Orthopedics. The head nurse looked in and offered a few words of welcome. But the young man was too exhausted and dazed to notice her.

Cherry instructed George, their ward orderly, who had changed Bob Smith into a hospital gown, to keep his ragged garments here until tomorrow. She wanted a chance to examine them carefully for any clue to his identity. For now, Cherry encouraged him to eat and to nap. Her efforts were useless. At three, when Cherry was scheduled to go off duty, she went to the head nurse.

"Mrs. Peters, I'd like to stay with Bob Smith. At least until he relaxes enough to eat or sleep. I could stay on duty straight through the evening."

"I know you're concerned for this patient, Miss Ames, but Dr. Watson says we'll give him medication to help him sleep. No, you'd better go home and get some rest."

Cherry wondered about her patient as she changed from white uniform into street clothes. Who was he? Where was his home? Where was his family, if any? What tragic happening had caused such distress that his memory was a blank? How could he be restored to the present?

Cherry went home and for the first time in her life did not say a word about her day's nursing work. Her parents and twin brother, Charlie, were astonished.

"Something special is happening," Cherry apologized.

That evening she took out her textbooks and looked up amnesia. "Functional amnesia is a *purposeful* forgetting of things too painful to remember. It is generally not due to any brain injury or disease, but is a memory disturbance. It is not faking or pretended illness; it is as definite and actual an illness as pneumonia."

Cherry closed her textbook. How did one cure a lost person who remembered nothing at all of his past? How did one solve a mystery with no clues?

CHAPTER II

Dr. Hope

CHERRY ARRIVED ON THE WARD AHEAD OF TIME THE next morning. Looking into Bob's room, she saw a big, blond man sitting with him. He was Dr. Hope, the head nurse said.

"He's been here for half an hour. Your Bob Smith seems to be talking to him."

"What's Dr. Hope like?" Cherry asked. She had never worked with a psychiatrist, and might not have a chance to do so now. She remembered that psychiatrist, literally, meant a doctor of the soul. "I should think he'd have to have a great deal of sympathy and imagination."

"Well, my friends the Websters live next door to the Hopes," the head nurse said in her practical way, "and they report that Dr. Hope and his two small sons are crackerjack tennis players and that the doctor groans like anyone else when it's his turn to mow the lawn."

13

Dr. Ray Watson came into the ward, said good morning to the nurses, and waited as anxiously as Cherry. It seemed like a long time until Dr. Hope came out of Bob's room. He looked very thoughtful, but he smiled when he saw Dr. Watson.

"It's not so bad, Ray. The boy is depressed, but he isn't so ill that he can't stay here. I'll recommend that. Of course I'll have our team of psychiatrists come over and examine him—today if they can make it. Personally, I feel hopeful for him."

"That's good, Harry. Glad to hear it."

"Not that we'll have an easy time. There's no guarantee we can help him recover his memory," Dr. Hope said. "But there's a good chance. Now, which is the nurse he talked to?"

Dr. Watson introduced the head nurse and Cherry, and Ruth Dale who was just coming in. Dr. Harry Hope shook hands with all of them and said to Mrs. Peters:

"Can you arrange for Miss Ames to spend extra time with this patient?"

"I'll get an extra nurse's aide, so that she can, Doctor."

Cherry was encouraged to have Dr. Hope accept her, even temporarily, as Bob's nurse. Dr. Ray Watson went with them to a staff office on this floor. There Dr. Hope began a briefing on how they all might best take care of the doubly ill patient.

"First, I think it will be easier for Bob Smith, or whatever his true name is, to have the same nurse—a nurse he already trusts—working along with *both* his medical doctor and with me. . . . Yes, here, Ray. . . . You can count on me to come to Hilton Hospital daily to treat him. He'll make better progress, I think, in your normal hospital surroundings than among our patients who are more seriously disturbed than he is."

Dr. Hope looked with penetration at Cherry. "What did you do to get him to talk?"

"Nothing, Doctor. I spoke softly to him—bathed his feet—that's all."

"Well, you did the right things. He wasn't very willing to talk to me."

"Could it be," Cherry suggested respectfully, "that he finds it harder to talk to a man than a woman—for some key reason?"

Dr. Hope grinned in pleasure and Dr. Watson said, "See, I told you she catches on fast."

Cherry felt pleased and embarrassed, and later fascinated by what Dr. Hope went on to say.

An amnesic like Bob Smith had thousands of fellow wanderers. Mental health authorities in all states were doing everything possible to help them and send them home. In past centuries they, and those with more serious mental illness, had been ignorantly regarded as willfully dangerous or evil, and thrown into dungeons and chained as criminals. This practice dated back to the Middle Ages when people believed that "demons" had "taken possession" of these unhappy persons. Now, Dr. Hope said, although the medical profession and the law recognized that a few psychotics might do dangerous or criminal acts, and must be restrained, the mentally ill were treated as any other sick persons and given medical care. He added that their suffering was bewildering and intense, perhaps harder to bear than the pain of physical illness. Nowadays, though, with good care, very many became well and happy and sound citizens again.

"About Bob Smith—"

Dr. Hope said that he was—unconsciously—forgetting certain *carefully selected* things in his past, things which he found impossible to face. These were the very things that he must be helped to remember, and to face and deal with. Dr. Hope's job would be a sort of detective work, to find these forgotten facts in Bob's clouded memory. To do this, he would use various uncovering techniques.

Dr. Ray Watson asked loudly the same thing Cherry was thinking. "Talking about detective work, why don't we call on the Hilton police force and see if they can help us? Of course they already know about the motorist's report, and they know we have an unidentified man here as a fracture case. But we haven't yet told the police this is an amnesia victim."

Dr. Hope hesitated. "Asking police help doesn't always work out. These amnesia cases can be surprisingly difficult. The clues and secrets are locked away inside the person. Making them ill, you see. However, we'll give the police a try, Ray."

"Bob probably will be able to remember unimportant things," Dr. Hope said. "It will be a start, at least. Miss Ames, I wish you'd carefully examine his clothes or belongings for any—what would the police call it, Ray?"

"Any identifying feature, I guess."

"Yes, I will, Dr. Hope," said Cherry.

She returned to Orthopedics, tiptoed into Bob Smith's room, and softly closed the door behind her. Her patient was dozing. Bob must have slept off his first exhaustion, for his thin face was a more normal color than it had been yesterday. But his breathing was rapid and shallow, and his hands twitched in his sleep, and he frowned.

"Nervous and upset even in his sleep," Cherry thought. She glanced at the chart and the night nurse's report: temperature normal, pulse 90 per minute, complained of headache; his movements were abnormally slow, a symptom of depressed feelings. Well, on his breakfast tray the teacup and plate were emptied; that was one good thing.

In the closet Cherry found Bob Smith's shabby garments and systematically searched them. No labels, no dry cleaner's tags, nothing in the trousers pockets. No leads, in short. In a jacket pocket, she found a small calendar for this year. Its pages were torn off up to April.

"April! This is September. Did time stop for Bob in April? Was it April when his memory blacked out? If so, where had he been in the six months since that date?"

Cherry tried the jacket's other pockets. . . . Empty . . . another empty . . . wait, there was something in the inside pocket. She pulled out a piece of thin white paper. A letter. There was no envelope, hence no postmark, and the letter bore no date. It was in a feminine handwriting, without a salutation, and was signed "S." It read:

"It was good of you to tell me what you did last evening. At the moment I didn't understand you. I hadn't realized that he's under such a handicap. Now I do and I *will* make allowances. So don't worry. S."

Cherry read the note again. It hinted at more than it said. Who was "S" and who was "he"? She suddenly felt Bob Smith looking at her. She was startled but maintained her calm.

"Hello. How do you feel this morning?"

Didn't he recognize her? He seemed to be in a hazy, dreamy state.

"Bob, I'm looking in your pockets for something to identify you. We're trying here at the hospital to help you."

He said weakly, "I know."

Good! He did recognize her! He did understand. Cherry thought of things to say to him—about bringing him back to the present, about sending him home. Better not. Maybe Bob Smith did not want to go home—or maybe he had no home. She could stir up a storm of emotions in him with a few wrong words. Talking, or forcing Bob to talk, could be as disastrous as giving a patient the wrong medicine. Better wait for Dr. Hope to lead the way.

"Bob, may I keep this note and the calendar?"

No answer. She took his silence for assent.

During the morning, Cherry made Bob comfortable, and applied cold compresses for his headache. Presently Miss Bond, a new employee in the Admitting Office, came in. She carried a ledger. She had been advised, evidently, to conduct the interview with Bob Smith through the nurse. He listened but would not speak.

"Can you give me the usual information?" Miss Bond asked crisply. "Name, age, address, occupation, names of any relatives?"

"I—I don't think that's available at the moment. Bob?" Cherry glanced at him. He looked away, dazed. Cherry shook her head at Miss Bond.

"Can you tell me," Miss Bond continued, "how and where the patient got hurt? Any previous illnesses? Shall we list him temporarily as John Doe?"

Cherry saw tears well up in her patient's eyes. He pulled the covers around him as if trying to hide. Cherry went to sit beside him and said:

"Miss Bond, will you excuse us now? We'll send the information to the Admitting Office as soon as we can."

"Well, it's most unusual—Oh, I see. Yes, surely, Nurse." Miss Bond left, red in the face with embarrassment.

For a few minutes Cherry held Bob Smith's hand in silence. Then he turned his head so that he could look at her.

"I'm sorry. All mixed up. I'm so ashamed."

"Don't be. It's all right."

"I can't even remember my own name. It's terrifying."

"S-sh, now. You'll remember."

Cherry waited. His breathing grew less agitated, more regular.

"Nurse? Miss—Miss Cherry?"

"That's right."

"I think I've been using the name of Bob Smith. I made it up. It sounded like a real name to me."

Cherry nodded and kept silent. His hand in hers relaxed, and then he fell asleep. She felt immensely sorry for this young man. Never had she seen anyone so lost and alone.

At lunchtime Mrs. Ball, who headed the hospital's Social Service Department, rapped and asked Cherry whether it would be advisable for her to see Bob Smith. Cherry hesitated about another interview. But she knew Leona Ball to be perceptive and kind, so Cherry said:

"Well, Mrs. Ball, come in but just say hello."

Mrs. Ball took a long look at the dazed man.

"No, I see I'd better not. Let me know what I can do for him—perhaps I could contact public or private agencies, or send out inquiries about him?"

"That would be a great help."

One further, long interview did take place that afternoon. The team of psychiatrists came, as Dr. Hope had promised, to give Bob a further examination, and see to what extent they agreed with Dr. Hope's first findings. Cherry was not present; she did her regular work on Orthopedics. After three o'clock, when the psychiatric team had gone, Dr. Hope called her into the staff office. He talked to Cherry privately.

"Well, it's agreed Bob is to stay at Hilton Hospital. Sit down, Miss Ames. Here's what happened in consultation this afternoon, so you'll have a clearer picture of our patient, and what you and I are going to do for Bob."

Cherry sat down, all attention. She watched this big, vigorous man pace around the office, stand still to think, pace, and then grin at her.

"Now isn't it reasonable for me to be disappointed that we can't interview Bob Smith's relatives? Relatives could fill in his life history, and tell us all sorts of relevant things. We always talk to the family first thing on admitting a patient—but with Bob, we don't even know if he's got a family. But we did take certain tests, and we'll do more."

The team of psychiatrists had given Bob, so far as his illness permitted today, a psychometric test that measured intelligence and the Rorschach "ink blot" test. The latter helped bring out ideas that troubled him, but only in a very general way. Later on, the team might take an encephalogram or brain-wave photograph. So far, the psychiatrists were satisfied that "Bob Smith" had sustained no brain injury or disease, had better than average intelligence, and had lost his memory because of some severe psychological upset. Exactly what had happened to Bob to cause this, and exactly how to treat Bob, was up to Dr. Hope to discover.

"We'll have to feel our way, at first," Dr. Hope said.

"We, Doctor?"

"Certainly. You're Bob's nurse and my assistant."

"But I'm not especially trained for this kind of case, you know," said Cherry. "I had one course at nursing school, of course—"

"The patient trusts you. You have imagination. That could be enough. At least I'm going to try you out."

Dr. Hope bent down and peered at Cherry.

"What's that worried look about? See here, better than fifty-five percent of so-called mental cases are temporary. After we help them analyze their problems and give them a few days' 'first aid,' they come to themselves and can go home." He laughed. "One man was brought in to our Mental Hygiene Clinic because he was standing on a street corner distributing dollar bills. Well, he was celebrating winning the sweepstakes, and he was always a generous man."

Cherry smiled, too. "I guess a sense of humor is going to come in handy."

"Not that Bob Smith is as mild a case as these. Yes, we'll need humor, and kindness, and a hopeful outlook. We must listen compassionately to whatever Bob says, and not pass judgment on him but try to understand. You and I will have to do our very best for him. We're the only people he has to help him."

"And he has me. I care about him, too." Dr. Ray Watson stood in the doorway. "Hope, do you intend to work at the University Hospital or at this hospital—or both?"

"Both," Dr. Hope said cheerfully. "This young nurse is going to do double duty, too."

Dr. Watson mumbled something about "Hard work and idealism never hurt anybody—only way to cure the patients." Then he said:

"By the way, I asked Leona Ball to telephone the police department. They're sending one of their detectives. Name of Hal Treadway. He'll be here tomorrow to talk to our mystery patient."

"Well, Miss Cherry," said Dr. Hope, "when you see the right moment, you'd better tell Bob that a visitor is coming to help him. Prepare him."

"I'll try, Dr. Hope."

CHAPTER III

First Steps

THE DETECTIVE'S FORMAL QUESTIONING ON FRIDAY distressed Bob Smith and yielded no information. That was not the detective's fault. Hal Treadway was an unobtrusive little man in sports clothes, perfectly agreeable to have Cherry and Dr. Hope in the room while he asked his questions. But Bob grew irritable. He broke out into a sweat and stammered:

"I don't know where I got the money to leave my hometown. Or anything! If I could remember I'd tell you."

"Take it easy, son," said the detective. "Try and think where your folks are. Where's your mother? Can you tell me *her* name?"

"I don't know! I mean, I haven't any family." Bob pulled himself up by the hand straps and sat bolt upright in bed. He was shaky and indignant. "If I had a family, wouldn't they be looking for me?"

23

"Not necessarily," the detective muttered, but Dr. Hope stood up to put an end to the interview.

"Sorry, Mr. Treadway, the patient can't tolerate any more direct questioning. We can't press him. Will you come into the hall with me? Nurse—" Dr. Hope indicated the enamel tray with its plain tepid water and sponge. "Take care of Bob, then join us, please."

"Yes, Dr. Hope."

Left alone with her patient, Cherry gently put cold applications on his burning forehead. She gave Bob another healing dose of silence and he quieted down. His eyes followed her as she lowered the window shades, then came back to the bed and turned his pillows over to the cool, fresher side.

"Miss Cherry? I guess you think I don't want to cooperate."

He sounded anxious. She reassured him.

"You see, Miss Cherry, I realize I'm in an odd condition. I've realized it for a long time. Though I don't know how long." Bob's brows wrinkled in his effort to grasp time. "Anyhow, all the time I was wandering and working at odd jobs—"

Wandering. Working at odd jobs. Cherry filed these bits of information away in her mind. These were the first leads Bob had mentioned.

"—I was afraid to talk to other people. Afraid they'd see how odd I am at present, and commit me to an insane asylum. I'm not insane." He looked at her pleadingly. "Am I?"

"No, Dr. Hope doesn't think so. The other doctors don't think so. You're ill, and you'll get well."

"I feel so alone."

Cherry took both the patient's hands in hers. "You're not alone. I care, and Dr. Hope cares, and Dr. Watson cares very much about you. We're going to give you our very best, skilled medical care. If you'll just trust us and work with us—"

"I will." Bob cleaned back and closed his eyes. "You're nice."

Cherry left him to drift off to sleep. She rejoined Dr. Hope and the detective in the hospital corridor. Dr. Hope was explaining to Mr. Treadway that contact with the police would only aggravate Bob's emotional upset, which accompanied and caused his amnesia.

"Don't you think, sir," the detective asked, "that if this boy doesn't like talking to the police, there might be a good reason for it? Apart from his—ah—state of mind, that is. How do you know he isn't mixed up in some crime?"

"We don't know," Dr. Hope said. "It's possible. Anything is possible, with an unknown person. But as I told you—"

"All right, Doctor, I'll work with Bob only through you and the nurse. I'll start right away to try to trace his identity and connections."

Cherry was curious about what methods Hal Treadway would use. Dr. Hope was curious, too.

"Well, while I'll certainly do all I can," the police detective said, "you have to understand what's involved in a case like your patient's."

In order to locate a missing person, or to identify a haggard, undoubtedly changed wanderer like Bob, required the cooperation of large numbers of police experts, long periods of time, long distances of travel, and often the almost endless study of great numbers of records.

"We have urgent cases like Bob Smith's turn up oftener than you'd think," the detective said. "But we're the Hilton police, and our first attention has to go to local cases and Hilton people. Unfortunately we haven't enough men, nor enough time and expense money, to conduct a detailed investigation on *every* missing persons case."

In Bob's case, Detective Treadway explained, he had no identifying features or scars as clues. He was just a nice-looking young man. At present he was so thin, wind-burned, and shaggy that he probably was hardly recognizable. As for the letter and calendar Cherry had found in his pocket, they revealed next to nothing. His blistered feet told rather more.

"From past experiences with these cases," the detective said, "I'd conjecture that Bob has kept moving."

"Kept moving," Dr. Hope repeated. "Of course that doesn't tell us whether he's wandered a long way from his home, or whether he kept moving within a limited area."

"The chances are that he comes from some distant part of the United States," Hal Treadway said. "Something inside them drives these wanderers."

The police detective promised to send out a teletype description on Bob to the police of other cities; to list him with the nationwide Missing Persons Bureau; to check his fingerprints with large agencies like Army, passport bureau, big employers, and civil service—at once.

"It'll take time for these people to check their files, though."

"Time!" Dr. Hope made an impatient gesture. "We can't afford to wait around. The patient could grow worse. This young man won't get well unless and until he can be helped to learn who he is. Then he'll have to remember what forgotten situation is troubling him. Otherwise—no cure."

Dr. Hope's warning registered with Cherry.

"We *can't* wait, Mr. Treadway!"

"Well, Doctor," the detective said, "I'll take Bob's clothing and try to find out, personally, whether it has any identifying marks, and if so, check these leads."

Cherry ventured to say that she had examined Bob's garments and found no markings or labels.

Hal Treadway told her, "There could be markings not visible to the naked eye. I'll examine Bob's clothing under our ultraviolet bulb. It's a violation of the law for a laundry or dry cleaning establishment not to mark garments, and I've never seen a worn garment yet that wasn't marked. When we hold Bob's jacket under the blue bulb, the chances are we'll see a series of numbers and symbols. Then I'll check those with the Laundry and Dry Cleaner Mark Identification Bureau, which has national coverage."

"Then there's some chance of immediate informa-tion?" Dr. Hope asked.

"If we're lucky. I'll check also with all local employ-ers who hire transient help."

Cherry brought Bob Smith's garments for the police detective to take with him. He promised to get in touch with the hospital people as soon as he discovered any-thing. Dr. Hope thanked him, but after the detective left, remarked to Cherry:

"The police procedures are going to take time, and it looks as if he can make only a limited investigation. I'm not satisfied. Are you, Miss Cherry?"

It surprised her to have this doctor turn to her so informally and ask her opinion. Still, she was a mem-ber of his medical team and he seemed to want to talk over with her anything that affected their patient.

"I should think all we can do," Cherry answered, "is wait and see what the detective can accomplish."

"Bob can't wait too long. I think we'll try our first Pentothal interview with him tomorrow."

Cherry knew that Pentothal was a drug, to be admin-istered by physicians, preferably in hospitals, and that Dr. Hope intended to use it as an uncovering tech-nique. He explained exactly how and why.

Whatever had happened to Bob, he resisted remem-bering it. Pentothal would relax him and help ease his fear of what happened—or what he feared was going to happen. Once relaxed, he would be able to break through his amnesia and recall a few facts about himself. Or so Dr. Hope expected.

"We'll have to be very easy and tactful with him," Dr. Hope told Cherry. "If we press him too hard, we'll only frighten him and he won't talk to us."

Cherry nodded. "Will you explain to him first what we're going to try to do?"

"Yes. And we'll tell Bob that we're making a record of what he says, and why."

Since there were going to be several interviews, Dr. Hope would need a record so that he could review details and, later on, grasp the picture of Bob's life as a whole. Bob's memories would emerge in a confused manner, Dr. Hope predicted, because Bob himself was ill and disorganized. Dr. Hope and Cherry would have to piece the bits together into some sort of meaning. In order to keep records, they would place a microphone in Bob's room; this would be piped to a tape recorder in the next room or in the closet. They would tell Bob about the microphone, and also tell him they would conceal it, so that the constant sight of it would not make him self-conscious and inhibit his talking.

Cherry was intrigued. This promised to be the strangest kind of sleuthing she had ever done—pursuing a man's forgotten memories of his past—and she commented on it.

"We'll have to explore two kinds of past with Bob," said Dr. Hope. "One is his *recent* past, because some recent shock or crisis or facing an impossible situation has brought on his amnesia. But a sound person can face a crisis and not go to pieces. It's fair to assume that in some

respect Bob has a psychological weak spot or injury—
and has had it for a long time. It probably goes far back to
some deep-seated distress in his childhood. So we'll also
try to help him remember into his *far* past."

"That will make our puzzle all the harder to piece
together," Cherry said.

"Yes." Dr. Hope smiled at her.

"And when we do bring his troubles to light? What
then?"

"*If* and when," Dr. Hope corrected her. "Then we'll
have to help him face his troubles. Sometimes it's a
question of straightening out mistaken ideas a patient
has. Sometimes it's a matter of supportive treatment,
giving the patient reassurance and strength to meet
some difficult situation. Or sometimes, many times,
the practitioner must do both."

"I—I'm not experienced enough for this case,"
Cherry said.

"Try," Dr. Hope said. "If it doesn't work out, I'll have a
psychiatric nurse from my own hospital work with me.
But I think you'll do fine."

Dr. Hope, of course, would take the lead with Bob,
and that would guide her. Even so, the delicacy and
complexity of the treatment left Cherry with some
qualms. In comparison, she found that the physical
nursing that Dr. Watson had ordered was simple.

For the broken leg, all they could do these first few
days was wait and make careful observations. In order
to be sure the cast was not too tight, so that it interfered
with the circulation and caused swelling, Cherry felt

her patient's toes to see if they were warm or cold. She frequently examined the edges of the cast and skin for pressure points and irritation. The cast itself was supported by pillows to keep the bones in alignment; pillows also provided Bob with other support. Cherry and the orderly helped him to change his position often; he had a light cast so that he could be moved and turned. This was important, for if the patient did not move or was afraid to turn, immobility could lead to slowing of his digestive processes, loss of appetite, bedsores, even some risk of pneumonia. Although Bob needed extended bed rest, Cherry knew how important it was to encourage him to turn and move, and to eat.

Bob's chart showed he was anemic, and he was a little irritable. But already he was improving, less exhausted, less panicky, after three days' bed rest and treatment. If only his sleep were not so restless, as the night nurse reported. . . . Cherry did not neglect her other patients, but her mind was on Bob.

When she came on duty the next morning, she found Bob Smith just waking up. He was cheerful and even whistled a little. She hoped that augured well for the Pentothal interview. Mrs. Peters suggested, "Leave his door open, so that he can see the other people on our ward." Cherry did so, and moved his bed so that he could look out. Bob watched with mild interest; elderly Mr. Pape and Tommy waved to him. But after half an hour his eyes took on that glazed, faraway stare again. Cherry closed the door. Well, he'd seen the ward and that was a start.

"Who's that young fellow with the broken leg?" the other patients asked. "Why is he in there?"

"Sure, move him in with the rest of us busted bones," Tommy said. "Everybody gets homesick in a hospital."

Mrs. Peters explained that Bob Smith had had a bad shock, and needed to be quiet and in a private room for a while. She, Ruth Dale, and the orderly knew more than that about his illness. There was no need for the patients to know, however; they might misunderstand. Dr. Hope wanted the other men to treat Bob naturally and easily, if he improved enough to be brought on the ward. Normal companionship could be part of his cure. If and when he came out of his long silences—if today's first uncovering technique would work—

That afternoon Dr. Hope went alone into Bob's room. Cherry presumed he talked to Bob, to prepare him for the interview, and administered the Pentothal. After an interval, Dr. Hope summoned Cherry.

She went into Bob's half-darkened room where a softly lighted lamp burned at his bedside. It was quiet, almost hushed, in here. Bob appeared to be more relaxed than she had yet seen him. His face was flushed and the pupils of his eyes were dilated, but he smiled at Cherry.

"Hello, Miss Cherry. I'm going to do my best."

"I'm sure you are."

She sat down in the chair beside Dr. Hope's, as he indicated, next to the bed.

"Would you like a cool drink, Bob? Chewing gum?" Dr. Hope offered them.

"No, thank you. I'm not thirsty. I just had a cool—" His voice trailed off.

"Just relax, Bob." Dr. Hope nodded and leaned back in his chair. He was unhurried. "You must have had a hard time. Can you tell Miss Cherry and me where you were just a few days ago?"

"I guess it was around here."

"Mmmm. What did the place look like?"

"Trees. Streets. People. No one I knew." Bob broke into a sweat. "Can *you* tell me what town this is? Hilton, I think you said, but what state?"

"Illinois." Dr. Hope answered as if Bob's question were a perfectly natural one. "Have you ever been in Illinois before?"

"Not that I know of."

"When I say *home* to you, what do you think of? Close your eyes and think. Take your time."

Bob made an effort. "A large white frame house," he said vaguely.

"I suppose that's where your family lives."

"I have no family!"

Dr. Hope nudged Cherry. She said pleasantly, hoping it was the right cue:

"Everyone has a family."

"Well, I haven't. I—I'm the sole survivor."

Cherry was inclined to believe him, but she saw a tiny frown between Dr. Hope's eyes. He said:

"Haven't you anyone at all? Who were your family members?"

"No one—no one—"

"Your father," Dr. Hope prompted. No answer. "And your mother. Where is your mother?"

Bob grew so distressed that Dr. Hope said:

"Never mind. Let it go for now. Unless you want to tell us why you believe you're the sole survivor?"

"I—My father is dead."

"Yes. How long ago?"

"While I was still in school. In college."

"I see. By the way, which college did you attend?"

Bob turned his face away. A minute went by. "I can't remember," he said painfully.

Dr. Hope said that was all right, he would remember everything in good time.

"And your mother?"

"She's dead, I tell you! How many times must I say so—I beg your pardon. Very rude of me."

Bob's excitement about his mother—he had replied calmly about his father—was not lost on either Dr. Hope or Cherry. Cherry smoothed over the bad moment by offering Bob a drink of water. He was glad of the lull. Dr. Hope resumed:

"Well, let's see now, Bob Smith. That isn't really your name, is it?"

"No, I made it up when I was in a town—around here, I think—and I was applying for an odd job in a—possibly a restaurant? The man in charge asked my name and—"

Dr. Hope nodded. "What is your name?"

Bob forced a grin. "I'd like to know that myself." For that much humor and courage, Cherry patted his hand.

"Miss Cherry?" said Dr. Hope. "You have a brother, I hear," and gave her the lead.

"Yes, a twin brother, in fact." She tried to think what events in her brother Charlie's life might be paralleled in any young man's life. "He's seen service in the Air Force. Have you been in the armed forces, Bob?"

"No, I haven't." He seemed entirely calm and certain about this.

"But you're the right age for it," Cherry said.

"Yes, but I haven't. I know when I was in my teens I went to a boys' summer camp and they taught us how to handle rifles—marksmanship—we had a shooting range—and I know that I attended college, because I remember the long quiet hours of study. But I haven't been in any of the armed services," he said very definitely.

This seemed unlikely to Cherry. She glanced at Dr. Hope for his reaction, but his expression was noncommittal, friendly.

"You're about twenty-five, I'd say, aren't you, Bob?"

"Twenty-six, I think, sir, if I've got the present year right."

Cherry told him the year, matter-of-factly, as if she were telling him the hour. Poor Bob was lost in time.

"Thank you," he said. "I wish I knew what date it was when I left home."

Cherry remembered the calendar she had found in his pocket, with the paper torn off at last April. She had better not mention it unless Dr. Hope did so. He chose instead to pick up another thread of Bob's remark.

"When you left home, you say. That was the large white house. Picture the house in your mind's eye, Bob, and tell me what feelings it stirs up in you."

Bob threw his arm across his eyes, and thought. When he took his arm away, he looked bewildered.

"I *know* there is something I should be worried about, but I can't remember what it is."

"You *know*? How do you know?"

"I just do. I'm sure of it. It troubles me."

"*It*?"

Bob said sadly, "I only know that I do—or rather, I ought to feel terribly worried and responsible."

"Some trouble about your family," Cherry murmured. "With the large white house."

"No."

"With what place, then?" Dr. Hope asked.

Bob sank back, tired. "I don't know. It just doesn't come clear to me. I almost see some place to tell you about, and then it's as if a wall of mist rises up."

"All right, you've done fine." The doctor signaled to Cherry that the drug was wearing off. "A good start. See if you can't take a nap now, Bob."

He was already dozing off.

Cherry tiptoed out after Dr. Hope. They held a brief conference in the hall. Dr. Hope held up one hand and counted off on his fingers what this first interview had yielded.

"First, Bob denies he has a family, but he recalls a white house and grows upset at mention of his mother. Very cloudy there. Second, he says he's been to college.

I'm inclined to believe that; he talks like an educated man. Maybe he'll remember or describe what college, and we can trace his identity through college records. Third, he's sure he never had military service, but can't explain why not. Yet he's the right age and physically fit. He probably was balanced enough until some unbearable stress caused this breakdown—"

Dr. Hope was inclined to believe Bob had had some military service but was actively forgetting it. Cherry reminded him that the detective, who had fingerprinted Bob, would check on that.

"Good. What else? Bob said he *knew* that he *ought* to feel concerned and responsible about something. And that 'something' is the crux of his present difficulty."

"Present difficulty—an injury rooted probably in his childhood?" Cherry asked, "Did I notice correctly that Bob remembered only the recent past in this interview? Didn't remember his far past at all?"

"Right! Bob remembered that he'd had odd jobs around here. As we'd expect. Now, if we or that detective fellow could locate his employers—"

Cherry made a suggestion, and Dr. Hope approved it. Their uncharted search was under way.

CHAPTER IV

Detective Work

THE NEXT DAY WAS SUNDAY. CHERRY'S MOTHER PROTESTED when she rose from the dinner table to make a special visit to Hilton Hospital.

"On Sunday afternoon, dear? I thought you were coming with Dad and me on the Garden Club's autumn tour."

"Please excuse me, Mother, Dad. I'd *like* to visit your friends' gardens with you this afternoon, and I hope everyone will admire your dahlias. But I—"

She hated to refuse, especially when Charlie was absent, too. This weekend he was driving some neighbors home from Lake Michigan with their young children and all their vacation gear. Mr. Lane had dislocated his ankle, Mrs. Lane was not a very good driver, and the Lane children were already late for the opening of school. Cherry thought for a moment how solidly all the people around her were rooted in family and neighborly ties. Imagine being Bob Smith, who had no one and belonged nowhere! Or at least so far as he knew. . . . Cherry looked at her parents and around the familiar, comfortable house. She felt a rush of gratitude.

In what rooms had Bob Smith grown up? Who were his parents, and did he perhaps have sisters and brothers? When his memory vanished, what house had he wandered away from?

"We must find that place and some of those people," Cherry told herself as she walked toward the hospital.

On her way she passed Hilton Clinic, a fairly new building downtown. Dr. Fortune, her old and good friend, was a senior staff member here. Dr. Fortune was enthusiastic about the Clinic and its group practice. Cherry had once worked there and liked it, too. Hilton Hospital, where she worked now, was an older and more extensive medical institution, located at a quiet end of town. Cherry walked on out there. This afternoon a great many visitors' cars were parked around the hospital's landscaped grounds. No visitors for Bob Smith, though, unless Cherry could count herself.

He was glad to see her. The relief nurse assigned to Orthopedics on Sundays was too busy to have much time for the young man in the solitary room. Glimpses of the other patients' visitors had made Bob feel forlorn and rather upset. Cherry talked to him, a little, very gently. Then she said:

"I'd like to take your picture, Bob."

"To help identify me? It's a good idea."

She had borrowed a camera from another nurse on this floor. The camera was capable of developing its own snapshots, without extra equipment, in a matter of two or three minutes. Yesterday she had devised this plan, won Dr. Hope's permission, and borrowed the camera.

"Smile," Cherry said jokingly to Bob. But he could not. She took three snapshots of him, and waited in silence while the camera developed them. "Have a look at them, Bob. Which one is most like you?"

"Is that me?" He was appalled. "Looks like a ghost. I've grown so thin. Malnutrition? I'd say, Miss Cherry, that none of them look much like me. Unless I can't remember my own face."

Nevertheless, Cherry took the snapshots downtown to the newspaper office. The editor was busy but willing to see her, and listened while Cherry told Bob's brief story.

"All right, I'll print his photo and story," he said. "But it's a long chance that someone who knows him will see it."

Cherry thanked the editor and left one of Bob's snapshots with him. She planned to give another one to the detective, and a third one to the hospital's social worker.

"I wish Sunday were over," Cherry thought as she walked back home. She was impatient for the next uncovering interview.

She reached her porch at the same time their postman, Mr. Marker, did. He handed her a special-delivery letter, postmarked New York. Cherry recognized the exuberant handwriting as Gwen Jones's.

Ever since she and several former classmates from Spencer Nursing School had leased the apartment in Greenwich Village, they had managed to stay close together—at intervals—in spite of nursing assignments that took them all over the country. This time, Gwen wrote indignantly, the Spencer Club members had been scattered for too long. She and Mai Lee were tired of living all by themselves at No. 9, and herewith called a reunion.

"Can you come for Thanksgiving Day? Can you come *any* weekend soon? Or can you come any old time? We'll be awfully glad to see you!"

Cherry wrote back at once. "I miss you, too. Have an urgent case, and don't know when I can come, but I *will* be there. Save your choicest nursing news for me. I have an extraordinary case to tell you about."

Bob had had a long sleep, induced by narcosis therapy, and awoke refreshed on Monday morning. When Dr. Hope came in for a talk with him and learned this, he was encouraged. Sleep often released memories in dreams and aided recall, he told Cherry.

"We're going to give him Pentothal again for today's interview," said Dr. Hope.

Today he explained a little more to Cherry about how Pentothal could help Bob "reach further" into his memories than without the drug. It is a relaxing drug that eases a patient's tensions and helps him to express freely his thoughts and feelings to the psychiatrist. It often helped the doctor to arrive at a diagnosis.

Dr. Hope prepared Bob for the midafternoon interview, and then asked Cherry to come in.

Leaving the active ward and stepping into Bob's hushed, shadowy room was like entering another world. The lamp glowed beside his bed. Bob had a trustful, drowsy smile as Cherry and Dr. Hope sat down with him. His face was in shadow, so that he was apart from them in a way.

"Let's start," Dr. Hope suggested, "with what you recalled last time. The large white house, and your family, remember?"

"Yes, I remember." A pause. "What did I say about working around here?"

They were surprised but prompted him, and after a short time Bob began to remember by himself. He talked at random, some of it disconnected or unclear, then his recall came into focus. He spoke as if half asleep, slowly.

"I found myself getting off a bus and walking on a road. Felt puzzled. Where was I? Who was I? Something was wrong, but what was it? Something extraordinary must have happened to me, I realized. I felt as though I might wake up at any minute and find the whole thing was a dream.

"I was on a country road, and there was a church nearby. I went into the churchyard and sat down to think. I found a letter and a calendar in my pocket. They didn't seem to belong to me. I remember trying to understand why I was hungry and dirty and unshaven, and didn't recognize the road—but I must have given up."

He stopped, and Dr. Hope asked, "Was this the first time you came to consciousness?"

"I think so. I'm not sure. The next thing I knew I was standing near the edge of a town. I had no idea where I was, or who I was. I began to be frightened. Then I saw how absurd my situation was, and I laughed—for a moment. I wondered if I'd died and was a ghost, if there are such things as ghosts. But I threw a shadow and my feet were sore and people stared at me curiously. I was shy of speaking to anyone. Afraid my voice might be odd, too.

"I saw a man with a newspaper and waited until he threw it away. I rescued it, and read the date on it, and learned of news events I hadn't heard of. None of it meant much to me, not even the date. I looked through the newspaper for news of a missing man, hoping it'd be myself, but there wasn't any."

Bob's voice trembled and died away. Dr. Hope let him rest. Cherry was careful not to speak or move, not to break the spell of memory. Bob sighed and went on:

"What was I to do? I had no money, no possessions, and I had to live. Had to get work of some kind, any kind, though I wasn't hungry or thirsty. Couldn't understand that. Besides"—Bob abruptly shifted to another subject—"I began to wonder whether my odd condition affected any people who knew me. Any family or friends or employers—though I couldn't remember a single person. I supposed that if I had anyone, they'd notify the police and make a search for me. But no one seemed to be on the lookout for me."

"So you assumed," Dr. Hope said, "that you had no family."

"I can't remember them, and apparently no one has searched for me. What would *you* think in my place?" Bob asked reasonably.

"You mustn't assume anything," Dr. Hope said. "There may be a search going on for you right this minute, but you've probably changed in appearance and you've probably kept moving around, making it hard to locate you."

"That's true," Bob admitted. "On the other hand there may actually be no family and no search."

Dr. Hope did not answer, cautiously, Cherry thought. It occurred to her that Bob might *not want* to remember his family. If he had one.

"So far, so good," Dr. Hope said, to encourage the bewildered young man on the bed. They talked a little more, but Bob was hazy and spotty in his recall. He remembered having had odd jobs—"I must have"—but was unable to tell Dr. Hope and Cherry where he had been going on the bus or when and where he had boarded the bus.

"Well, that's enough for today," Dr. Hope said. "I think we made important progress, Bob."

"You do?" He sounded listless, not interested. "I wish I could do better. Do I sound awfully—awfully odd to you?"

Dr. Hope shook his head and Cherry said, "You sound as if you've been trying your very best to pull out of this difficulty."

"I have, but I can't do it without help—your help, I mean." Bob's eyes closed in fatigue.

They left him to rest, and again held a brief summing up in the corridor. Dr. Hope explained to Cherry why today's recall was progress: at least some memories were coming clearly. Bob's inner barriers were beginning to dissolve.

During the next days, Dr. Hope worked again with Bob Smith. Bob tried hard, but on Tuesday he could remember nothing and on Wednesday he recalled only what he had already told them. Cherry felt as if they were up against a stone wall. It was a week since Bob had been brought to Hilton Hospital. She was glad when Mr. Clark, the visiting chaplain, came to sit with Bob for a while and comfort him. He needed all the love the hospital people could give him.

On her way home from the hospital late Thursday afternoon, walking as usual, she met Hal Treadway on Vermilion Street. The detective hailed her first.

"Glad to bump into you, Miss Ames. A little news. I've gotten a little way—not very far yet—by tracing the dry cleaner's mark on Bob Smith's suit."

"So there *was* a mark on his garments."

"Yes, an 'invisible' mark. The ultraviolet light showed it up. Have you a minute for a coke and a talk?"

"Have I!" Cherry knew the detective would report eventually to Dr. Hope at the hospital, but if she could bring his report sooner to Dr. Hope, so much the better for Bob.

Mr. Treadway had gotten to work immediately, once he discovered the mark and tallied it with the police Laundry Mark file. The mark led him to a wholesale dry cleaner, then to a retail dry cleaner, and then to the customer who had brought Bob's suit to be cleaned. She was a Mrs. Cook, living in Hilton. The detective visited her, but Mrs. Cook had never heard of Bob Smith.

According to her, this was an old suit of her husband's that she had contributed, after having it dry cleaned, to a friend in the next town, Glen Rock. This woman had asked for clothing to give to some of the poor men who worked for her husband occasionally at his restaurants, as dishwashers, window washers, bus boys. The restaurant owner's name was Field; he had three short-order places in Glen Rock. The detective reached him by telephone, and Mr. Field had agreed to drive over to Hilton and the hospital as soon as he could, to see if he could identify the amnesia patient.

"I'll report all this to Dr. Hope and Dr. Watson," Cherry said to the detective. "How soon do you think Mr. Field can come?"

"Can that young fellow stand seeing a visitor now?"

Cherry thought he could. They made tentative arrangements for early next week, depending on Mr. Field's convenience.

"But don't get your hopes up," the detective cautioned her. "Chances are that Mr. Field doesn't know any too much about his transient help."

"I understand. Thank you very much."

CHAPTER V

A Lead Turns Up

ANOTHER STEP WAS GAINED THE NEXT DAY. WITH THE aid, again, of Pentothal and sympathetic conversation, Dr. Hope was able to draw out from Bob a connected, lucid account of his recent past life. Bob was still slightly dazed, but his slowed movements were now nearly at normal speed and, best of all, he spoke with ease. In answer to Dr. Hope's questions, and a few by Cherry, he rapidly said:

That he had attended Oberlin College, majored in the sciences, and had been graduated from there in a certain year. That his home was in Ohio. That only last week, before the accident to his leg, he had been working temporarily in Hilton for a traveling circus as a roustabout. Bob even named the circus, the Sells-Zotos Circus, and said, "They're almost through with their summer tour. Right now, they're probably winding up the season at St. Louis."

All of this rang true. He was a changed man! Cherry felt so happy and excited at his new, sure recall that it took all of her self-control to sit there quietly during the interview.

Dr. Hope's face as usual was a friendly mask. But he must feel encouraged, too. As they were about to leave their patient, Bob said:

"Would you do something for me? You're investigating about me, aren't you?" They nodded. "Then would you try to find out what it is—what I—why I—feel so anxious?" He tried not to stammer. "I know I have something urgent—difficult—to attend to—On my conscience. But I can't remember what."

Dr. Hope reassured him that the three of them together would discover that, too.

Dr. Hope led the way into an unoccupied room where he and Cherry could talk. "Poor fellow. It's bad enough to have to face a *known* danger. But it's the unknown that really terrifies and overwhelms. Well, we'll check on these new statements of his as quickly as we can. We need facts."

"Yes, Dr. Hope," said Cherry. She had already reported to him the gist of her meeting with the detective. "What can I do now to help?"

"See the hospital social worker and ask her to write—no, wire or telephone Oberlin College. What can we do to check with the circus?"

"St. Louis isn't so far away," Cherry said eagerly. "My friends and I could drive over there this weekend."

"That's great!"

As soon as she finished her nursing duties on the ward, she went to see Mrs. Leona Ball in the social worker's sunny, plant-filled office with its open door. Mrs. Ball admitted Cherry ahead of others when Cherry sent in a note: "Amnesia patient—sort of an emergency."

"Oberlin College." Leona Ball wrote this down. "But how are we going to ask the college to trace its records for a man whose right name we can't tell them?"

A description of Bob; a snapshot; science major; year of graduation; these things the hospital could give the college. Leona Ball promised Cherry that she'd try to get an answer by Monday. She'd explain the urgency of the case and ask the college to wire collect.

That weekend Cherry and Sue and Bill Pritchard drove to St. Louis. At the city's outskirts they located the Sells-Zotos Circus, which had played Hilton. The circus manager looked at them in disbelief when they showed him Bob's snapshot and inquired about a man who had worked as a roustabout.

"Look, kids," he said, "I've never seen this man in my life. Who told you such a tall tale?"

"But the circus *was* in Hilton a week or two ago?" Cherry asked.

"Yeah, but we haven't hired any outside men this whole year. Naw, I never saw any fellow like the one you're looking for."

Cherry was stunned. Was Bob lying? Cherry didn't like to think so. From the very beginning, Bob had impressed her as a serious, responsible young man, despite his present state. Still—

On Monday morning the social worker brought in the reply Oberlin College had wired her. The college had no trace of a former student or graduate who fit Bob's statements and description.

"Of course," Mrs. Ball said, "with such scanty information, and the snapshot not like his earlier appearance, Oberlin may not have been able—"

"Don't blame the college," said Cherry. "The circus never heard of him, either."

When Dr. Hope arrived, Cherry reported these two failures. The psychiatrist was more interested than surprised.

"No, Miss Cherry, I don't think Bob told us lies. Not lies, but fantasy. There's one species of amnesia which is falsification of memory, and it generally occurs early in treatment. The patient weaves together things which actually happened—such as Bob's noticing the circus was here in Hilton—with things he only imagines happened. Or—correction—events which possibly *did* happen in his past. For example, Bob probably attented a college, though it wasn't Oberlin. Part of his memory disturbance."

"He said his home was in Ohio," Cherry remembered. "But his other statements proved false, so perhaps his thinking Ohio is his home is false, too."

"Perhaps or perhaps not. Let's go talk to him."

They told him, without blame, that his memories of the other day had proved to be fantasy, not fact. Dr. Hope explained that he told Bob this only in the expectation that he would try harder and do better.

"I will," Bob said. "It's strange. While I'm telling you things, I'm never quite sure whether it's the story of my personal experiences, or other people's that I half remember, or even a movie I've seen somewhere. Or maybe just something I'm making up. I don't honestly know."

Dr. Hope said there was nothing alarming or surprising here. Bob's subconscious mind developed these stories to meet the needs of the moment, and to cover up the actual situations which he found too painful or shameful to remember.

"But I *want* to remember. And I'm sure I *did* go to college."

By means of free association of ideas—encouraging the patient to talk freely at random, so that one idea or memory led naturally into another—Bob recalled a good deal more. The first names of two classmates at college; a chemical formula they had argued about all one term; his dream last night of someone's spaniel; a green-walled room in his grandparents' house where, as a child, he had enjoyed his first Christmas tree. However, these recollections shed no light on Bob's central problem, and, as Dr. Hope pointed out, Bob "selectively left out" the family members at the Christmas party. His mind blotted out whatever was really important.

"Why a chemical formula, Bob?" Cherry asked. "Did you major in chemistry?"

He thought hard. "Biochemistry, I believe."

"Whose spaniel was it?" Dr. Hope asked.

"Heaven only knows! We never had a dog at our house. My mother doesn't—" But he stopped.

Later that afternoon, after Dr. Hope had gone, a man named Westgaard came in, asking to see Bob Smith. He said he was a local farmer, and had seen Bob's photo with its "Who Am I?" caption in the newspaper. Today was the farmer's first chance to come to town. He stated that a man who might be Bob had done odd jobs for him last summer for about two weeks. Cherry warned Mr. Westgaard that Bob was ill, then took him into Bob's room.

"That's the fellow that worked for me," the farmer said. "Nope, I don't know nuthin' about where he come from. He worked pretty well but he was strange. Wouldn't say boo to anybody. Peculiar, dreamylike."

Bob did not recognize the farmer.

Cherry talked a little to Bob about the farmer and gradually jogged his memory. He recalled that he had wandered and had different jobs at different places.

"Some of them escape me. I walked endlessly. Must have been fourteen, sixteen hours a day, some days. I never begged, though, so far as I know. You can almost always get a job at some restaurant as a counterman or dishwasher. There was one restaurant man in particular who'd always help me out. What's his name? Can't think of the town, either. He'd always feed me, and let me wash windows if no other work was available."

"Mr. Field?" Cherry suggested. "In Glen Rock?"

"Field? Maybe that was it."

Cherry was excited when the detective showed up at the hospital late the next afternoon, bringing Mr. Field. The restaurant owner was a plump, kindly man with a shrewd glance. Cherry showed the two visitors into the staff office where Dr. Hope was working with Bob's tape recordings.

"Why, sure, I know Bob Smith," the restaurant man told Dr. Hope and Cherry. "Is it all right if I go in to see him?"

"Just a minute, please," the psychiatrist said. "We'll go in with you, and I think it may do Bob good to see you. But first, Mr. Treadway probably has something to tell us, privately, if you don't mind."

Cherry showed Mr. Field into an anteroom and said, "We'll just be a few minutes. Would you like to look at a magazine?"

"Ah—thanks. Miss Nurse? Bob Smith isn't that boy's real name, is it? He stumbled all over himself when I asked him his name."

Cherry explained about his loss of memory.

"Ah! So that's it! Well, let me tell you, he's an awfully nice boy. I don't care if he's been in trouble or prison or whatever—I don't ask questions of the men who come to me hungry and ragged and in need of work. They're unfortunates, and entitled to a chance to work."

Here, Cherry thought, was a compassionate man. She told Mr. Field they did not really know what had happened to Bob, and excused herself.

She returned to the office, where Dr. Hope was telling the detective what little the hospital people had learned from Bob during the past week. They had waited for Cherry to be present for Mr. Treadway's report.

"Not that there's much to report," said the detective. "The Missing Persons Bureau sent nothing but a negative report, so far. I sent Bob Smith's fingerprints to all the armed services, and they report no record."

"So he's accurate about never having been in the service," Cherry murmured.

"Mr. Field couldn't supply any leads, either. But I thought you'd want to talk with him. Now, Doctor, I have to say something I wish I didn't have to say. This is as much help as I'm authorized to give you. I'm a city detective, and there are a number of other cases waiting for me, and I can't put them off any longer."

Dr. Hope did not hide his disappointment. "Honestly, Mr. Treadway? Can't the Hilton Police Department let us have your services for a week or two longer?"

"I'm sorry, Doctor. If I get any more replies on these inquiries I sent out, I'll send them to you. And I'll keep my eyes and ears open for anything about your patient."

The detective bowed out, leaving them feeling rather helpless.

"Well," said Dr. Hope, "let's see what Mr. Field knows."

In the anteroom they counseled the restaurant owner that his visit with Bob had best be brief. Cherry went ahead to tell Bob that Mr. Field was coming, then the psychiatrist brought Mr. Field in.

"Hello, Mr. Field," Bob said, and held out his hand. "I'm glad to see you. Miss Cherry, this is the man I told you about—the man who always could find some job for me."

No doubt about it, he recognized Mr. Field and even better, remembered himself in connection with this man.

Mr. Field pumped Bob's hand. "Well, well, well!" he said, a shade too heartily. "What happened to your leg? We've missed you around the restaurants. Yes, sir, we certainly have." He swallowed hard.

Bob answered something vague and polite. He looked in Cherry's direction for help, and Cherry wondered how much he remembered of the restaurants or the people there. He smiled anxiously at Mr. Field from his bed.

"Well, Bob, you look to me as if you're in better shape physically, and in a whole lot better spirits—except for the leg, I mean—than the last time I saw you a few weeks ago." This much improvement was the first fruit of the hospital's efforts. "Yes, indeed, Bob, whenever you're ready for a job again, you come right back to me!"

Mr. Field was started on another booming speech. Dr. Hope touched his arm, and suggested he say good-bye for now.

In the anteroom Mr. Field mopped his forehead with a handkerchief. The visit to Bob had shaken him.

"I never realized the boy had lost his memory. I could see when he came around several times asking for work—anybody with eyes in his head could've seen—that the boy was hungry and unhappy and in some kind of trouble. But I never guessed—"

"Amnesia isn't an easy thing for a layman to recognize," Dr. Hope said.

"He was secretive," Mr. Field insisted to Dr. Hope and Cherry. "He didn't talk any more than he had to, to anyone. A nice boy, though. It struck me at the time—maybe you've noticed this, too?—that he has abilities far above his present situation in life. This Bob Smith is no tramp, he's an educated man, courteous, has a sense of duty toward other people—"

"Yes, Mr. Field," said Cherry. "We've noticed that, too."

"Though to be exact, we've had no chance to observe his sense of duty," Dr. Hope said.

"Well, I'll give you an example—Say, I clean forgot to show this to the detective fellow! My wife reminded me this morning. Hal Treadway's left, hasn't he? Too bad." Mr. Field dug in his pocket and took out a pawn ticket. "This will show you how conscientious Bob is."

Once last summer, when he was unable to repay a small loan from Mr. Field, Bob gave him the pawn ticket. So far as Mr. Field remembered, it was for Bob's watch. Mr. Field never redeemed the pawn ticket. When Bob wandered off, he saved it to give back to him in case he returned.

"Now I guess I'd better give it to you hospital people."

He handed the pawn ticket, which came from a Glen Rock shop, to Dr. Hope. The psychiatrist remarked on its date, last summer, and handed it to Cherry.

"I have a heavy caseload at the University Hospital, so I haven't time to look into this matter. Miss Cherry, can you take care of it?"

"This young lady can drive back to Glen Rock with me right now," said Mr. Field. "I could drive her to the pawnshop. Then she could catch the bus back to Hilton."

"That's kind of you," Dr. Hope and Cherry said in unison, then grinned at each other.

Since Cherry had completed her ward duties before Mr. Field's and the detective's visit, she was free to drive to Glen Rock now. Mr. Field turned out to be a chatterbox. Cherry managed to listen with one ear, but she was speculating about Bob. How had he managed, confused as he was by amnesia, not to beg but to find and hold odd jobs? Basically he must be a self-respecting, steady sort of man. His habit of responsibility toward others must be ingrained in him, too, to continue even in his time of stress.

After a half hour's drive they entered the tree-lined streets of Glen Rock. In a rather shabby section of the town, Mr. Field stopped the car in front of a pawnshop. It looked dingy, but respectable enough. Mr. Field was obviously in a hurry to be at his restaurants before suppertime. Cherry thanked him and said good-bye to him, entering the pawnshop alone.

She had no trouble in redeeming Bob Smith's ticket. The man behind the counter handed over, without comment or questions, a man's wristwatch. It was a good, standard American watch, in a stainless steel case, and with a simple leather wristband. Cherry waited until she was out on the street to examine it carefully. The wristband showed wear, and the watch did not look new. Unfortunately, there were no initials on the case.

"But there is a lead here!"

Cherry brightened as she remembered that every watch bears the manufacturer's name and a serial number. On the bus ride home to Hilton, she managed to pry open the back of the case with a hair pin. She found some letters and numbers, but they were too small to see clearly on a moving vehicle at twilight. At home she borrowed her father's magnifying reading glass and tried that. Yes, the manufacturer's name and the serial number were clearly visible.

Cherry copied them down. She would ask Mrs. Ball to write at once, on the hospital's letterhead stationery, to the watch manufacturer. This was a large firm in New England. With any luck at all, the manufacturer should be able to supply the name and address of the retail shop where Bob's watch had been bought. Then, by writing there, it might be possible to learn who—

"Cherry!" her mother called from the dining room. "Aren't you coming in to dinner? Dad is ready to serve you."

"Are you nursing or sleuthing out there all by yourself?" Charlie asked.

"Both, you might say," Cherry replied, and she came to take her place at the family table.

CHAPTER VI

Picture Tests

"YOU NEVER KNOW WHAT TECHNIQUE DR. HOPE IS GOING to use next," Cherry said to Mrs. Peters next day. The head nurse was curious and concerned about their special patient. "He telephoned and told me he's going to try TAT pictures today—and said we're not to give Bob any drugs or medication."

"TAT pictures?" the head nurse asked. "Is that a test or another uncovering technique?"

Cherry shook her head and her dark curls danced under the white cap. "I'd imagine it's more of Dr. Hope's special brand of sleuthing, wouldn't you?"

"Well, describe it to me when you find out. And I wish to high heaven that you'd tell Tommy and Mr. Pape and the others something more about Bob. It's all Ruth and George and I can do to keep the ambulatory boys from going in to visit him."

Cherry laughed. "Dr. Watson told me the men are curious. You know, he booms and thumps around so, Dr. Hope told him to take it easy with Bob."

"How *is* that boy coming along?" the head nurse asked.

"Better, Mrs. Peters. He's trying awfully hard."

"So are you, Cherry. I've noticed you're putting in overtime hours."

Dr. Hope came in just then, and the head nurse excused herself.

"Ever seen TAT pictures, Miss Cherry?" the psychiatrist asked her, just outside of Bob's room.

"No, Doctor."

"Well, they are carefully designed drawings that show, or rather suggest, all sorts of situations. The patient's reaction to them reveals what's shrouded in his mind. Not literally, but it gives the psychiatrists hints or clues. You'll see how it works as you watch and listen."

"Is it really a scientific method?"

The big, blond man grinned. "You mean it sounds like guesswork? No, it isn't. The Thematic Apperception Test—that's what TAT stands for—has been worked out experimentally by psychologists at universities, using large numbers of tests and patients. There's a scale of interpretation that works as accurately as the intelligence tests or vocational aptitude tests. TAT pictures are a standard tool in many mental hospitals. Satisfied, now?"

"Yes, Dr. Hope, but what do you want me to do?"

"Just be there. You're a soothing influence for Bob, as it happens. One thing. Show you're interested, encourage Bob to talk, but be neutral about anything he says."

Dr. Hope rapped at the door, which stood partly open. "It's us. We're bringing you a kind of game."

Bob called cheerfully, "Come in."

Dr. Hope explained to Bob, "I'm going to show you some pictures, one at a time, and ask you to make up as dramatic a story as you can for each."

"I? I can't make up stories, Doctor," Bob murmured.

"The pictures are exciting, they'll suggest stories to you, you'll see. I'd like you to tell what has led up to the scene shown in the picture, and describe what is happening at the moment—what the people feel and think—and what the outcome will be. Do you understand?"

Bob nodded. He was becoming interested.

"Since you have fifty minutes for the ten pictures, you can give about five minutes to each story. Here's the first picture."

Dr. Hope handed Bob a picture that might have been a good-sized postcard, not in color but in black and white. Dr. Hope glanced at his wristwatch while Bob studied the first picture. Cherry could see that it showed a boy of ten or twelve in a living room, holding a violin. Behind him stood a woman, and further back in the room, a man. There seemed to be someone else present, or it might have been a shadow. No one in the picture was defined very clearly; it all was dreamlike, suggesting something moving and troubling here.

"Come on, Bob," said the psychiatrist. "Just tell the first story that comes into your head."

"Well—that's the boy's parents with him, the mother wants him to go on with his violin lessons, but his father thinks she indulges the boy. Farther back in the room, that's the boy's brother, listening to them argue."

"Very good. How does the boy feel?"

"I guess he feels that he's causing a family argument—makes him feel a little out of the family circle—"

"How does the brother feel?"

"I—I don't know. Unless—Maybe he doesn't like it that the younger brother receives so much attention from their parents. It's just a story I'm making up, you understand?"

This was as much as Bob would or could say on the first picture. Dr. Hope remarked pleasantly, "Good try," and handed him the second picture.

For each shadowy, haunting scene presented to him, Bob told stories with only a little strain. In some cases his stories made no immediate sense. Cherry noticed that the stories were disconnected and did not link up with one another—at least not on the surface. She could not tell whether any single story stood out significantly. One or two pictures made him smile.

Then Dr. Hope gave Bob the ninth picture. Bob reacted excitedly. It suggested—at least to Bob—a place on the water, sandy, rocky, on rough water—a place near the ocean, not inland like Hilton—with big jutting rocks. A few shadowy figures seemed to be walking there. Evidently something important and troubling had once happened to Bob in such a coastal place, for he broke into a sweat. The psychiatrist urged him to talk.

"This is where the boys go to swim," he said. "It's a place where accidents can happen. Because of rough water—and because in heavy weather, it's hard to see all those rocks, especially when fog envelops them."

"How many boys, Bob?"

"Just two boys."

"Is one of them you?"

"It might be me," Bob admitted.

Dr. Hope asked him what sort of accident it might be. Swimming or sailing or just climbing and slipping on the rocks, Bob said vaguely. Near which ocean was this spot? Of all the TAT cards, this beach scene absorbed him the most. Yet Bob was too agitated to answer. He could not remember where, he insisted.

The psychiatrist let the question go, and offered him the tenth picture. By this time Bob was tired, and could tell only a sketchy, desultory story. Dr. Hope put the ten pictures away. The fifty minutes was up. He praised Bob's cooperation, and said:

"Tomorrow or next day, we'll do the next ten pictures."

"Oh, gosh," Bob said, and laughed a little. "That's work. How many more pictures are there?"

"Only the ten more. Weren't his stories interesting, Miss Cherry?"

He had, in fact, conjured up extraordinarily vivid scenes. In private with Cherry, Dr. Hope said he was encouraged by today's try. "He put his finger on a family consisting of father, mother, and two sons—and he described the family attitudes of each one of them."

"And that scene on the rocky beach—"

"Yes, that's a clue, too. An accident there involving the two boys, somehow. We'll follow up these leads, Miss Cherry."

The session cost Bob something, though. After Dr. Hope left, Dr. Watson noted he had a slight return of the stammering and physical slowness, and a tendency to stare. He had the orderly, George, give Bob a relaxing warm sponge bath and a back rub. Then Cherry brought him some warm broth.

"Dr. Hope said it would do this boy good," Dr. Watson boomed to Cherry and Mrs. Peters, "to visit with the other fellows on the ward tomorrow. Isn't it about time? That doorway is wide enough for us to wheel out his bed."

Cherry and the head nurse asked Bob, the next morning after breakfast, how he would feel about being wheeled out onto the ward. "For a get-acquainted visit," said Mrs. Peters. "The other men would like to know you. They're a friendly group."

Bob looked terrified for an instant. Cherry told him that he wouldn't have to stay any longer than he wanted to, and that Dr. Hope thought some companionship would be a good idea. Bob still hesitated.

"If I could be of any use to anybody," he said. "In that case—"

Mrs. Peters picked up his cue. "Sam Jones, who's broken his right shoulder, mentioned that he'd like to write a letter this morning. If you could write Sam's letter for him—?"

"I'd like to do that," Bob said. "And maybe the other men won't find me odd."

Cherry was delighted with the way the entire ward welcomed him. Disabled temporarily themselves, the men were subdued, sympathetic company for Bob. He smiled from his bed at young Tommy who rapidly rolled over his wheelchair to shake hands. The orderly rolled Bob along between the double row of beds, while Cherry performed introductions. Bob looked with pity at the long-term spine patient, who said cockily, "Today's the day I try my luck at sitting up. Maybe next week I'll be walking around on crutches." Bob nodded, but he was unable to find words. Old Mr. Pape, resembling a snail in its shell under the cast that protected his broken hip, waved to Bob.

Cherry bent and whispered, "Want to go back to your room now?"

"No. It's interesting here. They're nice," Bob whispered back. "But why do they have to wear those faded, pinkish bathrobes?"

"The hospital budget can't afford quite everything."

"But those old robes are dispiriting. Maybe I could buy new bathrobes for the ward."

He suggested it so matter-of-factly that Cherry saw he meant what he said. It sounded as if, in his usual life, he might be a man able to afford this act of generosity.

By propping a notebook against his good knee, Bob managed to write the letter that Sam dictated. Cherry noticed his handwriting: it was small, neat, exact, like the script of a scientist, and he printed all the capital letters. She noticed, too, when she came by with a tray of medicines and chemicals that he seemed to know a good deal about them.

"Who is this young man?" Cherry thought. "He seems to be highly trained in the organic sciences. Wonder what his work is—and where?"

All of a sudden he grew tired and had to be taken back to the quiet of his room. It was too bad, because Mr. Pape was having his sixtieth birthday today, and the volunteers in their blue smocks were just bringing in an immense birthday cake, to serve at lunch. Bob received a piece, anyway, complete with a candle. He enjoyed being part of the life of the ward; that was a hopeful step in his recovery.

On Friday, the following day, Dr. Hope came again. He had given Bob a chance to rest, and now they would attempt the next ten TAT pictures.

Again Cherry lowered the shades and turned on the lamp, so that Bob's room was half in shadow. Dr. Hope sat down beside Bob's bed, with Cherry seated nearby, and started to talk casually. Any outsider would have thought these three people were three friends having a visit, and so, in a way, they were—except that each of their "visits" had so much at stake.

Bob started bravely on the first of the next ten pictures. Here were two or three people in a meadow at dusk, moving toward each other—or were they going away from each other?—and far away over the hills, someone was coming. For this picture, and for the next four, Bob drew from the turmoil inside him curiously troubling, revealing stories.

He was startled when Dr. Hope handed him the sixteenth card. So was Cherry. It was blank.

"But I can't—What do you want me to tell?"

Dr. Hope said, "I'd like you to imagine a picture, describe it to Miss Cherry and me, and then tell us a story about it as you've done for the other cards."

"Well, it's in an office. Not in an office building—in a factory, more likely. Two men are quarreling." Bob hesitated. "They're very angry with each other. Especially the older one." He stopped dead.

"Can you tell us who they are?" Dr. Hope prompted. "Partners, friends? Or perhaps what they're quarreling about?"

Bob looked confused. The direct question had upset him. He stammered and lapsed into silence.

"Never mind," the psychiatrist said gently. "It's an office, and the two men are quarreling."

"Yes. The two men are quarreling. Accusations, denials. Someone's guilty."

Cherry and Dr. Hope listened acutely. They did not dare interrupt with questions at this point.

"They shout at each other—it's in an office—

Bob rambled on and grew incoherent.

"That's enough. Next card," Dr. Hope said briskly, to bring Bob back to himself.

"Oh. Yes. Well, let's see." Bob drew a quivering breath and composed himself. "This picture shows a farmhouse, or maybe it's a country inn—"

His storytelling for the last of the cards was uneventful. Again Dr. Hope praised and encouraged him at the session's end. Bob gave him a quizzical glance.

"You know, it's rather hard to take this game seriously, Doctor. The times before, when I talked to you sort of half-asleep from the injections—I found it hard to take all that seriously, too. I can't see how it can help bring back my memory."

"It's a technique that works," Dr. Hope assured him. Bob listlessly picked at the blanket. "You want to get well, don't you?" Bob nodded, without enthusiasm.

"Perhaps he's just fatigued," Cherry suggested to Dr. Hope after they left Bob's room.

"No. That unwillingness to regard his memories seriously is a facet of his unwillingness to return to the real world. He's fled from his troubles by forgetting them and he doesn't wish to return and face the bad situation he fled."

"I noticed," Cherry said, "that he never mentions the future. The other day when I mentioned planning for his future, he lost his temper."

"That's right. Hasn't the morale yet. But he will. He's improving."

Dr. Hope discussed today's session with Cherry. She sensed that he did it to instruct her, and to fix the points gained by stating them aloud.

"Two men quarreling. One is older than the other. The older one is the angrier of the two. Why? Hmm."

"Is one of them Bob, possibly?" Cherry asked.

"Possibly. We don't know. Remember, Bob's stories are a mixture of fact and fantasy. All of it revealing."

Cherry reminded Dr. Hope, "When Bob told the 'violin' story, he mentioned the younger brother with the violin and the older brother who sort of envied him. Could the two men quarreling be the two brothers, grown up?"

"I thought of that, too," Dr. Hope said. "But we mustn't leap to conclusions. Keep our thinking fluid. Now. The two men make accusations and denials, but Bob said 'someone' is guilty. Who is guilty? Is one of the two men guilty? Or is it a third person?"

Cherry saw there was no point in asking about a dozen questions that came to mind. Dr. Hope and she, somehow, must secure the *facts*.

The psychiatrist promptly took the next step.

Late that same Friday afternoon he returned to their patient. Cherry waited outside Bob's room. It was late; she wore her street clothes, and knew that her friends expected her within the hour. She, Bill, Sue Pritchard, and Joe Hall planned to drive out into the country for supper, on a double date, in this still-mild, last week of September. Cherry counted back on her fingers. This was Friday the twenty-sixth; Bob had been admitted to Hilton Hospital on Wednesday, September tenth; he had been under treatment for a little more than two weeks. He was better, but how few identifying facts they had discovered!

Dr. Hope came out of Bob's room. He beckoned to Cherry and spoke rapidly.

"I reminded Bob of the stories he had told for the twenty TAT pictures and asked him to fill in certain important details. Also, I asked him to look back and say which stories came from his own experience, or a friend's experience, or a book, or a movie. Not that the source of the story detracts—the patient selects certain key details to emphasize, anyway—but it'll help us to know that the quarrel and the seashore incident are facts."

"Or so he said," Cherry murmured.

Dr. Hope grinned. "Or so he said. Also, I asked Bob which were his favorite and least favorite pictures. He likes best, the one of a white house or homestead, and he likes the seashore scene the least. He seems to believe those are actual places."

"Were *is* that house? And that coastal beach?"

"He gave no hint. Unless they exist only in Bob's imagination. . . . There's a second step to follow up on these TAT pictures, and that may tell us. But I'm detaining you, Miss Cherry. No, I won't tell you the next step until Monday." He laughed. "Run along home and have a good weekend, and forget all about hospital matters."

"As if I could! Or wanted to." Cherry wished him a happy weekend, too, and ran down the stairs since the elevators were full.

On the way down she almost collided with Mrs. Leona Ball, who was coming up the stairs to find Cherry. The social worker waved a letter.

"The watch manufacturer answered our inquiry! I thought you'd be here late as usual, so I—Look here!"

The watch manufacturer stated that the watch bearing the given serial number had been sold two years ago to the Jennings Jewelry Shop in Cleveland, Ohio.

"Do you suppose the shop has a record of *their* customer for Bob's watch?" Cherry asked. "Because if they have—" She was almost afraid to hope. If they had, she would at last have a definite, recent clue as to who Bob Smith was.

"I'll write to Jennings Jewelry Shop before I leave the hospital today," Leona Ball promised, "and I'll send it air mail."

CHAPTER VII

What Bob Recalled

AT SEVEN A.M. ON MONDAY CHERRY WAS ON HER WAY TO her ward, reporting in with dozens of people in white. She said good morning to dietitians, doctors, therapists, nurses (she didn't know everybody's name, but that didn't matter), and to nonmedical hospital people in blue: secretaries, guards, a few volunteers who were here this early. In an hour or two the secretaries, laboratory researchers, clerks, and still others would come in.

"What a special, skilled, wonderful world a hospital is!" Cherry thought. "Next to my family, I love this place best." She knew her mother understood, but her father and Charlie grumbled good-naturedly that medical people formed a closed fraternity.

Just this weekend, when the Ameses had driven over to Dr. Fortune's cottage, to take him and his young daughter Midge for a drive, they had been unable to pry him loose from his discussion with Dr. Harry Hope.

Cherry was delighted to see "her" Dr. Fortune, who was a medical doctor and researcher, talking so earnestly with "her" psychiatrist. She'd known they were acquainted—through the hospital and the Hilton Clinic, and especially because in a small town like Hilton people knew all their neighbors. She had listened to them talk, and Cherry had grasped how closely the mind and the body interlock. After that, she felt she'd soon feel as much at ease with the psychiatrist as she did with the physician who had brought her and Charlie into the world.

Dr. Hope liked and admired the older Dr. Fortune. He told Cherry so this Monday at work.

"I could give you reasons in detail, but we'd better talk about what I plan next for Bob Smith. It's the next step even if the watch manufacturer's letter"—which Cherry had just reported to him—"leads us to some tangible information. You see, any actual facts the watch people may supply, such as Bob's name and address, are important, very important, but they aren't enough by themselves. We have to unearth what Bob himself *thinks* and *feels* about these facts. Now, this is how I propose to do it—Where's the tape recordings of the stories he made up for the TAT pictures?"

"On the machine. I put them on in case you'd want to play them back and study them today."

"I do, and I want you to listen to them with me." Cherry was a little surprised. "This is the next step I wouldn't tell you about last Friday."

Dr. Hope grinned at her, and Cherry grinned back comfortably. There was no more "witch doctoring" about treating mental disturbances than there was about nursing Bob's leg fracture and secondary anemia through their progressive stages. The next step was this:

Dr. Hope and Cherry would pick out from Bob's TAT stories those key words which he had used most frequently, or used when he grew upset or excited. From these words that were significant the psychiatrist would construct a word association test. "These words really are keys to what's troubling Bob, and they can further unlock his memory."

They listened together, and chose the words or phrases *accident, large white house, I can't, perhaps, quarrel*, and several others. Dr. Hope asked Cherry if she could contribute anything further from her observation of their patient.

"Well, from my conversations with Bob, I noticed he seemed familiar with medicines and chemicals." Dr. Hope added the words *medicines* and *chemicals* to the list. "I'd guess chemicals especially," Cherry said.

Dr. Hope said he needed to give more thought to the word association test, and admitted he had worked on it during part of the weekend. He telephoned the University Hospital to say that he would remain at Hilton Hospital all day today, and locked himself in Dr. Ray Watson's office with the tape recordings and plenty of paper and pencils.

Meanwhile, Cherry performed her regular ward duties. The long-term spine patient actually was able to sit up in bed and reach for a brand-new pair of crutches. Every patient in the ward watched and was heartened, and Mrs. Peters had George wheel Bob in for a look, too.

"Congratulations," Bob said.

"Thanks. You'll get well, too."

When Dr. Hope was finally ready, Bob's bed was rolled back to his room, and the three of them met in Bob's room as usual.

This test, too, was like a game. Dr. Hope had a long list of words that, he explained casually to Bob, he would fire one after another. Bob was to answer "off the top of your head—no fair stopping to reflect" with the first word or phrase, or situation, that occurred to him. Bob looked dubious but folded his hands and paid attention.

"White house?"—"Home." "Chemicals?"—"Business." "Mother?" Hesitance, then, "My fault." "Necessary?"—"Handicapped." "Quarrel?"—"No!" "Brother?"—"Accident." "Can't?"—"Can't."

To an outsider the word test between doctor and patient would have sounded like gibberish. But to Cherry, who from the beginning had heard every word of Bob's shaky recall, a dim pattern began to emerge. After the word test was over, Dr. Hope encouraged Bob to talk.

"Now what was that about a business?"

"A family business," Bob said.

"Yes. A business in chemicals?" Dr. Hope suggested.

"That's right. We supply manufacturers of so-called miracle drugs. We're not one of those huge chemicals manufacturing firms, such as you find in the Northeast and in California. We do have, however, a special formula which my father developed—patented the process—and we're the only ones who can supply it."

Cherry was amazed at Bob's full, revealing speech. How clear and alert mentally he was becoming! She leaned forward to listen.

"Is your family business located in the Northeast?" Dr. Hope asked. No answer. "In California?"

"We've lost the business."

"You have? Well, then, where *was* it located?"

"There isn't a business any more, I tell you," Bob said irritably.

"Yes, I see. Do you want to tell us how it was lost?"

Cherry remembered Bob's description of two men quarreling in an office. He said now, unwilling, "I guess the business failed. It must have been that. It's vague to me."

Here, Cherry realized, was an area of his life that Bob was deliberately forgetting. That pinpointed some part of his difficulties. Dr. Hope said in a conversational tone:

"You're trained in chemistry, aren't you? Biochemistry, too?" Bob nodded. "I suppose you were in the family business, then."

"For a while."

"Bob, now you remember yourself at college, working in the laboratories. You're wearing a white lab coat and when you look out the window at the campus, which college do you see?"

Bob thought hard. "I see it, all right, but I can't recall the name." He voluntarily described what he saw in his mind's eye, but that place could have been any one of dozens of peaceful green campuses throughout the United States.

"Who else was in the family business?"

"My father, and he's dead."

Cherry suggested, "What about a brother?"

"No brother! I haven't any family."

That clashed with his story of two boys on a beach where some accident had occurred. Indeed, the story of a family business was inconsistent with his heated assertion that he had no family. Here, too, lay a sore point.

Bob surprised them by rapidly retracing the years of his childhood and early teens. In an outburst of talk, he told of a happy childhood in a seacoast place, but of something important, troubling, that happened just before he entered his teens.

"Was it an accident?" Dr. Hope suggested. "Involving those two boys?"

Bob opened his mouth to answer when the ward telephone started to ring. It rang persistently; Bob was sidetracked. He sat up, listening to the phone.

"That might have been Susan on the phone!"

"Which Susan was that?" Cherry asked.

Bob scowled. "I never did tell Susan. Didn't feel I had any right to."

Susan! This sudden first mention of someone named Susan surprised both Dr. Hope and Cherry. Was Susan the "S" of the note found in Bob's pocket? The psychiatrist asked Cherry to get the note and read it aloud to their patient. She did so.

"Doesn't make any sense to me," Bob protested.

"Maybe I do know a Susan, but at the moment I can't think who she might be."

Another fact blocked off, hence it could be a key fact. The notepaper was still crisp and fresh. That suggested that "S" or Susan had written to Bob fairly recently. Bob's being a member of a family business must have been fairly recent, also, for he could not have been out of college for many years. So his "trouble area" was recent.

"What does Susan look like?"

"I don't know any Susan, Doctor."

"All right, then, what does your mother look like?"

Bob laughed. "What is this, another game?" He was stalling, evading—though not on conscious purpose. The psychiatrist, unruffled, said: "Well, if you'll describe your mother's room, maybe you'll 'see' her in it."

Bob described a lady's nicely furnished bedroom in minute detail, but he did not describe the lady herself. That effacement was significant. Even if his mother were dead, as Bob had once insisted, much too excitedly, he should be able to visualize her. He had some troubling reason not to.

"Imagine," the psychiatrist said, "that now you are walking out of your mother's room, and you go downstairs to the living room. It's evening, just before dinner. Who's in the living room?"

"Nobody."

"What time did your father generally come home for dinner? Didn't he and perhaps someone else come in about now?" Bob looked baffled. "How many places are laid at the dinner table?"

"I *am* searching in my mind, Doctor, but all I get are distant pictures of the beach and the rocks, from when I was small."

"Fine. We'd like to hear about the beach, too."

"The beach—well—" Bob sighed. "I'm so tired. Can't we have a recess, now?"

"All right," Dr. Hope said, "let it go. I think you told us a very great deal today."

"Are you going to send me home—when you find out where my home is?"

"If you don't want to go home, we won't force you to go."

"Thanks, Doctor. Though I suppose I ought to—it worries me, if only I knew *what*—"

Bob's eyes closed in exhaustion. They were about to leave him alone when Bob suddenly said:

"I'm beginning to recognize myself."

Out in the corridor, Dr. Hope and Cherry shook hands.

Dr. Ray Watson was satisfied, after another X ray, with the way Bob's fractured leg was healing. Bob had been doing push-up exercises in bed to strengthen the triceps muscles in his arms for the use of crutches. On Tuesday Dr. Watson said:

"Well, young fellow! What would you say if I told you we'll let you try your luck with crutches? Yes, sir, three weeks in bed is enough."

Bob grinned. "How soon can I drive a car?"

"Hear that, Miss Cherry?" Dr. Watson boomed. "Ambitious, isn't he? Well, we'll try you out on crutches first."

Bob's spirits rose still higher when Cherry brought him a pair of crutches. Standing up, he was taller than she had estimated him to be. At first Bob hobbled around his room uncertainly on the crutches. Cherry was interested to observe his scientific habit of mind as he figured out how best to manipulate them. He got the hang of them quickly, and said:

"Mind if I show my friends on the ward that there's another fellow around here on his feet?"

"Just wait while I ask our head nurse."

Mrs. Peters was happy to say yes, and Dr. Watson himself made a loud announcement to the ward patients. Bob hobbled forth to smiles and cheers from the men in casts and wheelchairs and braces.

"Congratulations," called Tommy and Mr. Pape and the spine case, who had his own crutches next to his bed.

Bob actually blushed and stammered when he said thanks. He stayed with his ward friends for lunch. This socializing was progress too. Cherry had to urge him back into his room.

Next morning Mrs. Leona Ball came into the ward. She was all smiles. The Cleveland jeweler had answered her urgent letter of inquiry about Bob's watch. The jeweler's letter read:

"Dear Mrs. Ball: Our business records show that a man's wristwatch of Excelsior make, #8991374, was sold two years ago this July to a Mrs. Olivia Albee. The customer paid for it with a check drawn on the First City Bank of Crewe, Connecticut. I myself waited on

Mrs. Albee and from our conversation had the impression that she was on a trip. She produced identification from Crewe to validate her check. I trust this is the information you require. Sincerely yours, R. J. Jennings."

"Albee!" Cherry exclaimed. "Mrs. Olivia Albee. Is she Bob's wife or mother or sister—or just a friend?"

"Or an aunt or grandmother," Leona Ball teased her. "I suppose if the jeweler had any more information than this, he'd have sent it along."

"It's a real lead," Cherry said. "At last we have the name of someone who probably knows Bob, and we have the name of that person's town. We'd better ask Dr. Hope's advice on what to do next, don't you think so? He'll be in tomorrow."

"Think again, Bob," Cherry said gently.

Bob was sitting up on the edge of his bed, legs dangling. Dr. Hope had assigned her to reveal the news to their patient; after so many pressing interviews, he felt Bob might be on guard with him.

"Think, now. Doesn't the name Albee sound familiar to you?"

"Albee . . . Albee . . ." Bob repeated. "And you said the town of Crewe, Connecticut. No, I don't think so—but it's confusing. It rings a bell somewhere. I think I once had a schoolteacher by the name of Alsop. Sure you don't mean Alsop?"

"No, I mean Albee. Is that by any chance your name?"

"Albee? No." But Bob looked very doubtful.

"You're sure, now?"

Bob sighed, rubbed his forehead, restlessly swung his good leg. Cherry waited.

"You're right. My name *is* Albee, Richard Albee. And my hometown is Crewe." His face cleared.

"You're sure of *that*, now?"

"Yes, perfectly sure. Go ahead and check. You'll find I've got it straight this time."

He was so calm and confident that Cherry was ready to believe that he was Richard Albee, of Crewe. Still, his earlier, calm statements that he'd attended Oberlin College and had held a summer job with the circus turned out to be fantasies.

"We-ell. And who is Olivia Albee?"

"My mother. She bought me that wristwatch—by the way, thanks very much for returning it to me. She bought it a couple of summers ago while she was traveling in the Middle West. In Cleveland, I think she said."

"Is Crewe your mother's home, too?"

"Yes. I mean it *was*, while she was still alive."

The subject of the patient's mother was a touchy one. Cherry gingerly decided to turn the interview over to Dr. Hope at this point.

He came in promptly, after Cherry's quick briefing. Bob seemed a little troubled to see him. He picked up the interview where Cherry had left off. Bob protested.

"I suppose you're going to ship me right back to Crewe—maybe write a note to my mother first. 'Here's your son, madam, he's on your hands now.'"

"No, we'll do nothing of the sort. I've told you that already, Bob. Or Richard?" Dr. Hope smiled at him.

"Relax. I'm still your friend. But I'm sure your mother or other relatives must be worried about you."

"My mother is dead, and I've already told you *that*."

"So you did," Dr. Hope said quietly. "I don't like to pester you with questions about her. I realize it's painful for you—but it's part of your cure."

Bob muttered, "I can't go back there, I can't!"

"Why not, fellow? What's bothering you?"

"Why, how could I ever face her?"

"Your mother?" No answer. Or did Bob mean the unknown Susan? Dr. Hope rephrased his questions.

"Yes, she's dead. Yes, recently! I don't know how recently! Well, she died of a tumor, it was neglected, the operation was put off too long because of—" He choked on his own words. "My mother was neglected, and she died."

"Bob, listen to me. Is your mother really deceased, or are you only *worried* that she may die?"

Bob's eyes grew shiny with tears and he would not or could not answer.

Cherry said, "You know, Bob, if your mother, or anyone, needs medical care and can't afford to pay for it, there's always free care available. Every hospital does that."

"That's right," Dr. Hope said. "Can't some other member of your family arrange for an operation if she needs one?"

Bob mumbled, "No other members in my family."

"Haven't you a brother?" The other boy on the beach, the other boy in the violin scene, the other man in the quarrel. Literally true or not, these scenes pointed persistently to two boys or two men, and Bob had admitted one might be himself. "Have you a relative named Susan?"

"*I* haven't. Oh, let me alone! Please. I haven't any family." Bob tried to suppress a sob. "Don't you suppose I'd tell you their names, or our home address, or our business address if I could?"

The inconsistencies in what he'd said hinted at many sorts of hidden facts. But Bob's panic was the urgent matter at the moment. Dr. Hope stood by while Cherry soothed him. They promised him they would find out all they could from Crewe, to help him remember. They promised to inquire discreetly so that Bob would not be thrown back into an obviously distressing situation.

At Dr. Hope's request, the hospital social worker wired the Crewe police, for a confidential report. Had they any record of a Richard Albee? Of an Olivia Albee? She gave what information they had about their patient, and in her long telegram also requested the Crewe police *not* to tell the Albee family (if one existed) of the Hilton Hospital inquiry just yet, because of medical reasons.

Mrs. Ball sent the telegram on Thursday. No reply arrived on Friday. Cherry made a special trip to the hospital on Saturday. No reply. She wondered how she could wait through the weekend.

CHAPTER VIII

Long Ago and Far Away

"JUST THINK," MRS. AMES REMARKED. IT WAS SUNDAY AND they were all at home. "A week from today is Columbus Day. And you, Miss Nurse, haven't yet had a vacation this year."

Cherry's father lowered the sports pages of the Sunday newspaper. "I should think any nurse would need to get away from shop talk, and have a vacation and enjoy a little social life."

"I do have a social life," Cherry said indignantly. "Or sort of one." She looked around for Charlie to corroborate this, but Charlie was absorbed in studying the want ads for aeronautic engineers. Either a new job or a promotion at his present Indianapolis job was his objective. "I went to Dottie Wilkinson's party last evening, didn't I? With George Baker, as Mother asked me to."

"George is a very nice young man," said Mrs. Ames.

"Yes, he is, Mother. I've known him since we met in the first grade and he still fails to interest me."

Her father asked? "Where's your old friend, Wade Cooper?"

"He's overseas on a job."

Cherry hadn't much patience or interest these days in parties or even seeing old friends. The need to solve Bob Smith's riddle—or Richard Albee's?—allowed her no rest. Later on, she told her family, she'd make up for this period with plenty of fun and good friends.

As if on signal, the telephone rang for Cherry. The operator said New York was calling, and then Gwen Jones's voice came on.

"Aren't you *ever* coming to swell the ranks of the Spencer Club?"

"Of course I'm coming. . . . I don't know *when*. With this special case. . . . Well, when I can get there. . . . How's Mai Lee?"

"We're all fine, Josie Franklin and Bertha Larsen got here Wednesday. . . . Well, I *did* say so. . . . In my letter. . . . What letter? . . . Wait a sec. Josie!" Cherry waited while one Spencer Club member conferred with another. Gwen's voice came on again. "The letter is still in Josie's coat pocket. Anyway, all I said is hurry up."

"Yes, ma'am. I know an order when I hear one. What's going on that's so special?" Cherry asked.

"Not a blessed thing. Just a visit and a gabfest." Gwen gave a sample—all their recent news.

The operator cut in. "There will be an extra charge for the next three minutes."

"Ouch! Cherry! I'm going to hang up."

"Save a bed and a hamburger for me," Cherry said, and hung up, laughing.

Of all things, on Monday morning at the hospital Cherry found Dr. Hope poring over a map. Then she saw that the map showed the northeastern states and included Crewe, Connecticut. Crewe was not far from New York City, Dr. Hope explained, about an hour or two by train or car. It was one of a cluster of suburban towns that dotted the shores of Long Island Sound. Across the water from Crewe's Connecticut shore lay the narrow strip of Long Island, on whose other side the open Atlantic pounded. The Sound itself was fed by the Atlantic Ocean.

"I've been sailing and swimming up there," Dr. Hope said. "The waters of the Sound are really treacherous at times."

"That's where Bob's accident with the two boys happened—if he's not making up the story."

"If he is, remember it reflects his feelings and 'stands for' the truth in his mind." Dr. Hope put away the map. "We might try to find out whether there *was* an accident, because now we have some new information to work with."

"We have?" Cherry's hopes leaped up. "Did the Crewe police answer, Doctor?"

"We're in luck. Look at this!"

He handed her a telegraphed report from the Crewe police department. It had reached Hilton Hospital late Sunday evening. It stated that a family by the name of

Albee lived in Crewe and had been in business there for many years. The Albee firm manufactured chemicals and medicines and had been founded by the father, Justin Albee, deceased for some four years.

"So Bob's father *is* dead, as he said!" Cherry exclaimed.

"Yes. But read the rest of it."

The Albee family at present consisted of the mother, Mrs. Olivia Albee, and two sons, Richard and Merrill. Richard had been gone from Crewe for about six or seven months.

"His mother *is* alive! He does have a brother!"

"Yes."

"Six or seven months—that was last March or April," Cherry figured. The calendar in his pocket had its pages torn off up to April. "So he broke down in April—I mean, *perhaps*," she amended as Dr. Hope cocked his head at her. She continued reading the Crewe police report.

Six months ago, Mrs. Albee had asked the Crewe police to send out a Missing Persons Bureau inquiry on Richard. However, the other son, Merrill, advised them that Richard had left voluntarily and there was no cause for alarm. Merrill told the Crewe police, in confidence, that Richard was under some cloud of a personal nature and wanted to be left alone for a while. The Crewe police department had therefore sent out a routine inquiry, as Mrs. Albee requested, but had not made any detailed investigation.

Bit by bit, carefully, Dr. Hope and Cherry imparted this information to Bob. They started by telling him that they had received good news about his mother: she was very much alive, despite his fears, and still residing in Crewe.

"She is? How can you be sure?" he asked.

They told him about the Crewe police report.

Bob seemed relieved to learn of his mother, yet not nearly as relieved as they might have expected. He did not want to talk about her. Dr. Hope did not press. He changed the subject, and then, casually, mentioned "your brother Merrill."

"Oh, yes, Merrill." Bob's expression was vague, then his face clouded. "Merrill. My older brother. That's right. He's all right, isn't he? What does the police report say about him?"

"Nothing of particular interest," Dr. Hope said. Cherry knew Dr. Hope must have some reason for evading. "Suppose *you* tell us something about Merrill. Well, Bob?"

"I guess you'd better call me Richard," he said gravely.

"Very well, we will. Now, about Merrill?"

Bob—or Richard—smiled. "He'd be amused to see *me* weaving around on crutches. Oh, he wouldn't gloat or anything, he'd be sorry, he's such a good guy. But, you see, *I've* always been the athlete, the—Merrill calls me the eager beaver."

Cherry heard an undertone here that she could not understand. She asked whether Merrill did not go in for athletics, too. Or for chemistry.

"Merrill?" Their patient sounded surprised. "Oh, no."

Bob—or Richard—spoke in unrelated snatches. Then he began to remember more consecutively.

"I can see the walnut highboy in our room, when we were boys, and I remember the arguments Merrill and I used to have about who could use the top drawers. The more convenient drawers. Now it's coming clearer. Merrill used to tell me—you know the way a kid brother gets teased—that I was the baby and shorter, so the bottom drawers had to be mine. Forever and ever, he said. Then when I shot up a head taller than Merrill, he said that I still ought to give him the preference—in everything, always—because of—"

Bob—or Richard—half laughed, remembering, but Cherry and Dr. Hope were listening closely.

"Because of what?" Dr. Hope asked.

The question was painful. Richard paled, wet his lips, but could not speak. Cherry started to prompt him but the psychiatrist gestured for her to be silent.

"Won't you tell us? Was it perhaps because of your mother, in some way? Or because of some accident or quarrel? You remember, don't you?"

Richard breathed hard. "It was—Just another boy. It was just a boy at the beach."

Cherry remembered Richard's agitation when he made up a beach scene for the misty TAT card. Another boy? That suggested in his boyhood.

"How would another boy know?" Dr. Hope asked.

"It *was* another boy."

"Unless perhaps it was your brother?"

"No." Richard turned his face away and refused to say more.

"Well, tell us something else, then. Was Merrill in this difficulty, too?"

"Please leave Merrill out of this."

Dr. Hope approached the sore point via another route. "Something extraordinary must have happened," he said gently.

"Something terrible happened. I'm sure of that much. Because I've never stopped feeling unhappy and guilty about him."

"About your brother?"

"No, you mustn't blame Merrill. Not for anything."

"You're fond of Merrill, aren't you?"

"Yes, very fond of him. He's my older brother. Four years older than I am. I've always looked up to him. But I—Funny I can't remember exactly what happened— but I feel as if I've done Merrill some lasting injury, and have to make it up to him."

It was plain to Cherry and the psychiatrist, from Richard's agitation about Merrill, that there was a good chance Merrill had been the "other boy" involved in the unnamed difficulty. Equally plain, Richard resisted telling anything much about Merrill, out of some feelings of guilt toward his brother. Some very tangled relationship must have existed between the two boys—and what was it now, between the two men?

Guilty, Richard said. . . . Was the guilt imaginary or valid? Did it apply to their boyhood or to as recently as last April? Guilty of what? Whatever had happened, in Crewe or elsewhere, whatever other persons were involved—his brother, his mother, Susan—the truth was locked away in Richard's memory. It was as if his memory had jammed, like a stubborn, complex piece of machinery, and all three people in this hospital room struggled to pry it open.

Under Dr. Hope's gentle questioning, Richard remembered a few things about his brother, and his family. He recalled his father.

"I'm sure our father *meant* to be impartial," Richard said hesitantly. "I'm sure he made every effort."

Dr. Hope raised his eyebrows. "But he wasn't?"

"Oh, he only favored Merrill a little, sometimes. Maybe I'd have done the same in his place. Merrill never was as strong as I am—not that Merrill ever complained. He's a remarkable person." He spoke kindly, devotedly of Merrill.

"Why wasn't Merrill as strong as you?"

"In a way it was my fault."

"How?"

"I don't remember."

The story sounded pretty thin to Cherry. Apparently it did to Dr. Hope, too. He put questions, with tact, about the boys' mother.

"She's the best mother in the whole world. But after what I did—I mean, after what happened to Merrill— After that, I felt my parents might never really want me. Especially my mother."

"You mustn't feel that way," Cherry said. "Weren't your parents good to you? Affectionate?"

"Oh, yes!" In answer to the psychiatrist's question, Richard said, "I was about ten or eleven when all this happened." He would not or could not say what "all this" meant.

"So you kept the incident to yourself," Dr. Hope said, "whatever it was, and nursed your feeling that you were at fault."

"Yes." And this psychological wound, like any physical wound that is hidden and ignored, had festered. It was still painful, judging from Richard's eagerness to change the subject.

Dr. Hope talked for a while about the family business, or his deceased father's business—Richard was unclear on this. Again he could remember only that the business concerned the manufacturing of medicines and drugs. Cherry had observed Richard's evident training in chemistry and biochemistry, from time to time, in conversation with him about the drugs that Dr. Hope administered to him.

"Did you take part in the business?" she asked. "Or did you plan to?"

Richard grew upset and protested he could not remember. This, too, was pretty thin. He apologized, saying he realized there were periods for which he could not account.

"Was Merrill in the family business?" Dr. Hope asked.

Richard had no recall on that, either. Apparently the business was another sore point. That, Cherry thought, brought the focus of Richard's distress up into the recent past. A question occurred to her. She gestured to Dr. Hope, then said:

"Richard, I don't understand what drove you away from home *now*. If you had foolishly run away from home when you were eleven and get all upset over that incident—well, some youngsters do foolish things. But why did you leave your home *now*—so many years afterward? Last spring, according to the police telegram. What drove you away?"

Richard grew agitated. This point, too, he could not remember. That is, he could not bear to remember his point of breakdown. But what was it? What had happened?

The only response their patient was able to make, out of his locked memory, was to repeat over and over that he was "guilty." Especially regarding Merrill and his mother. He could not name what he had done, or not done, except to blame himself.

"He's still badly upset," Cherry thought, "in spite of all progress."

In conference after the interview, Dr. Hope commented to Cherry that everything Richard had said tallied with the Crewe police report. But the report was all too brief.

"We need more facts," Dr. Hope said. "We need to know what the patient feels guilty *about*." He explained that guilt, actual or imagined, could have caused

Richard to break down and wander away. The psychiatrist needed the actual facts; then he could help Richard sort out facts from fantasy, and resume his life. That was the only way to help their patient get well.

"Couldn't we simply send Richard home?" Cherry asked. "Wouldn't he remember everything once he got there?"

"I'm afraid not. Restoring Richard to his family and home will not necessarily cure his amnesia." Dr. Hope said patients had been returned to their homes and continued to be amnesics. "You see, Miss Cherry, if there's family trouble, and that's what drove him away, then our restoring Richard to his family might *intensify* his loss of memory. No, that won't do. Our problem is to cure Richard and then reintroduce him into his family on *happy* terms. And for that, we need to know more about his relationships with his mother, his brother, the business, and the rest of it."

"We need more facts," Cherry mused. "It looks as if somebody will have to go to Crewe."

"It certainly does. That detective fellow—Hal Treadway—can't go. I can't go, too many patients at the University Hospital. Miss Cherry?"

Harry Hope looked down at her and Cherry looked up at him. They eyed each other, then burst out laughing.

"I see we understand each other," he said. "You're elected. Can you go?"

"If that's an order, Doctor, I'll make it my business to go."

"Well, I think it's part of your nursing job on this case. I also think you're a good person to do it—you're thoroughly familiar with the case and know what to look for, better than anyone but I would. A hired detective might get the facts but overlook the meanings. We haven't funds to hire a detective, anyway. I'll tell Hospital Administration and Mrs. Peters all this when I ask for time off for you from the hospital."

"How soon do you want me to start?"

"The sooner the better. We can't go any further with Richard until we have more facts. By the way, Miss Cherry, I don't know how we'll finance this trip of yours."

"I have friends I can stay with in New York, Doctor." She meant the Spencer Club's apartment. With luck she might borrow Gwen's car to drive up to Crewe. "As for the fare from Hilton to New York and back—the midnight coach flight isn't very expensive, and I've been planning to visit my friends in New York, anyway."

"Honestly? Well, I feel better about it, then. Let's see. This is Monday. Maybe some fast telephone calls will arrange things—"

Dr. Hope offered to pay out of his own pocket any incidental expenses Cherry might incur. She thanked him but said that except for a few restaurant meals, these would not come to enough to matter.

"You're an awfully good person to go."

"I've been looking for an excuse to visit my friends in New York, Dr. Hope. This trip won't be exactly a vacation, but it certainly should be interesting!"

They agreed not to tell their patient where Cherry was going, since it might distress him. Dr. Hope would tell him just before Cherry returned—bringing back what unsuspected information?

The hospital authorities promptly gave permission for Cherry to take a few days' leave from the hospital. Mrs. Peters rearranged the schedule: Ruth Dale, two volunteer teenagers, and she herself would double up on Cherry's ward work. Cherry telephoned Hilton Airport for flight information. And an hour later, when Mrs. Ames came home, she found Cherry in her bedroom packing a suitcase and wearing her gray suit.

"Cherry! Now what? I've learned never to be surprised by your impulsiveness but—You never said a word!"

"Didn't know till now, darling. Will you or Dad drive me to the airport for the eight o'clock plane? I'll explain at dinner."

At eight Cherry boarded the plane to New York, leaving her astounded parents waving out the car window. A few hours later Cherry roused the astonished Spencer Club nurses out of their sleep.

"I'm here," Cherry announced. "I told you I was coming. Isn't anyone going to say hello?"

CHAPTER IX

Cherry Asks Questions

THE SPENCER CLUB REUNION LASTED FAR INTO THE night and started up merrily again at breakfast. But Gwen and Mai Lee had nursing jobs to report to. Josie had a job interview to go to, and Bertha had promised to shop in New York for her numerous farm relations. The rush for hats, coats, and the front door started all at once.

"At least my jalopy is going to Crewe with you," Gwen apologized to Cherry.

Cherry jammed on her hat. "I wish I could spend the day visiting with all of you."

"We'll visit tonight," Mai Lee promised. The dainty Chinese-American girl urged the other four out of the door. "We'll all meet here at dinner this evening."

"At the Witches' Cave," Josie said. She was a rather timid girl, but she had a passion for murky, candlelit restaurants.

"We eat dinner at home," Bertha ruled. Since Bertha was a fabulous cook, no one argued. They called good-byes to one another, and the nurses wished Cherry good luck on her extraordinary search in Crewe.

Nearly a two hours' drive out from New York City brought Cherry into the quiet suburban town of Crewe, Connecticut. White-pillared churches, white houses with pumpkins set on their doorsteps, and the many schools and libraries reminded Cherry she was in New England. She drove along under Crewe's flaming autumn trees, remembering the poem about New England's "stern and rock-bound coast."

"Well," she thought, "I'm looking for 'a stern and rock-bound coast.'"

Her plan was to go first to the rocky beach that Richard had described with so much unexplained agitation. It had seemed to both Dr. Hope and Cherry that of everything Richard recalled, the unnamed, disturbing incident at this place was most important to Richard. That is, if such a place actually existed. She'd better inquire.

Cherry pulled in at a gas station and asked the young man in coveralls if he knew of a beach on rough water, which had big jutting rocks.

"Sure, miss. Probably you mean Gull Point."

"Is that a public beach, or private property, or what?"

"It's a public park and beach. It's open April through October."

She followed a bus marked "Gull Point," and after passing scattered cottages and sandy marshes, she saw from a cliff the open waters of the Sound. It was gray, churning water today, rough and angry looking. Cherry drove downhill into the park, past rows of closed bath-houses. At the edge of the empty beach she parked the car and got out. A salty wind flapped her hair and coat wildly.

She looked around rather anxiously for other people. Some workmen were repairing a dock. Cherry saw a weather-beaten elderly man wearing a park attendant's cap, and hailed him.

He was chilly and glad of a chance to step inside a shelter and talk to Cherry.

"Yes, ma'am, I'm the caretaker at Gull Point Park, all during the season. Sam Beasley, that's me. I'm a fixture here. Been working in this park for over twenty years."

"I'm glad to meet you, Mr. Beasley. I'm Cherry Ames, and I need some information from you."

He was eager to oblige. Cherry asked whether this beach happened to have any large, jutting rocks. For answer the caretaker led her out of the shelter into the wind and pointed far down the beach. She saw jagged gray rocks, taller than men, towering out over the water's edge. The crags tallied with what Richard had visualized from the vague TAT picture. So he had remembered this place as it really was.

"Mr. Beasley, you've been here for many years—do you by any chance remember the Albee brothers?"

"Albee brothers? Why, of course I do! There's an Albee family been living in Crewe for years, same as me. Crewe is the largest town around. The Albee brothers ain't boys any longer, though. It's twelve years, maybe fifteen, since the two of 'em used to come down to the Point, in summer vacation from school. Yes, fifteen years, every bit of it."

Fifteen years ago, Cherry figured. Richard had been about ten or eleven years old. Let's see. He was about that age, he'd said, when "something terrible happened."

"What were the Albee boys like?" she asked curiously. "Or maybe you don't remember. After all, you've seen thousands of boys at Gull Point."

"I know them well," the elderly man asserted. "I'll tell you this. I never saw two brothers more different from each other! Different as night and day. Even *before* his mishap here at the beach, Merrill never was—"

"So there *was* an accident!" Cherry exclaimed.

"I'm coming to that. I have to admit I liked Richard a whole lot better'n the other one. Most people did."

The park attendant said that Richard, though four years the younger, outstripped Merrill in strength, abilities, handsomeness, and pleasantness of disposition. Merrill was a nice enough boy, but Richard outshone him, effortlessly. Richard was not even aware of this. He looked up to his older brother. Merrill, though, seemed jealous of the younger boy. At the beach and in the water Merrill showed off, making the most of being four years older.

"I'd say Richard was around ten years old, and Merrill maybe fourteen, when he had that bad time in the water."

"Merrill?" Cherry asked. "Not Richard? Was it Richard's fault?"

"Now look, young lady. Who's telling this story, you or me?"

Cherry grinned, apologized, and listened.

Merrill, when a teenager, occasionally undertook feats at the beach that his younger brother could not manage. He often teased Richard in front of their friends. One day he and Richard swam far out and raced each other. It was the last week in September and the beach was officially closed, so there were no lifeguards on duty.

"I don't know whose idea it was to race, miss," the park attendant said, "but it was a fool stunt. I was on shore and I could see Merrill was having a hard time to swim back. Richard swam up to him several times, I guess to try to help him, but Merrill wouldn't have it. A couple of us swam out a ways, wanting to help him, but Merrill motioned us to go back. Well, he wasn't in any real danger, just tired, and anyway Richard was alongside him, so we did go back. He made it back to shore, finally, all spent.

"And then, if you please, for all that Merrill was shaking all over and could hardly stand up, I heard him bawl Richard out—in front of their friends, again—and argue with the little fellow. Maybe Merrill felt ashamed of making a poor showing. Honestly, I never in my life saw such an expression as on the little fellow's face."

"What expression?" Cherry asked.

"Well, Richard was all bewildered and close to crying. And that ain't all," Mr. Beasley said. "After that, Merrill contracted rheumatic fever."

Cherry knew that rheumatic fever, or inflammatory rheumatism, could start from prolonged exposure to dampness or from an infection, with children especially susceptible. She pitied Merrill for it is an extremely painful disease, and it often leaves the victim with an impaired heart. Even with good care and long rest, complete recovery is difficult to achieve. A person who has had rheumatic fever must cut down on his activities so as not to overstrain his heart. That must have been hard for a boy of fourteen, just growing up.

"Merrill was sick for a long time," the park attendant continued. "First at the hospital, then at home. He never got really well. The experience sort of changed him, too. He never had Richard's nice, friendly disposition, but after that, Merrill—Well, he was hard to get along with."

From Mr. Beasley's halting account, Cherry understood that Merrill had become a sickly, complaining boy. He had demanded special privileges and often blamed others for the results of his own shortcomings. He had been unable to go in for sports, and he did not care to take much part in other activities. As a result he had few friends. Except for Richard.

"You have to give Richard credit," Mr. Beasley said. "He was the most devoted brother you ever saw. Even when Merrill wasn't easy to live with. Lots of times—I live in Crewe, so I know—lots of times Richard would stay home with him, or give up good times to stay with Merrill, just because he felt sorry."

"Do you think that was because," Cherry asked, "Richard felt responsible or guilty about Merrill's accident?"

"He didn't have any reason to feel guilty, for heaven's sakes! Merrill struggled back to shore by himself— when he *needed* help—to make himself look superior to Richard. Still—well, yes—I suppose you could be right. Kids get funny ideas in their heads—grownups do, too, for that matter. I do know that Richard felt bad that he grew up big and strong and won the track meets and played on the school baseball team, while Merrill had to sit on the sidelines."

"So possibly Richard did blame himself, in some obscure way." This might be the reason—or *one* reason—for her patient's guilty, troubled feelings. Then Cherry asked, "Did Merrill *have* to sit on the sidelines? Couldn't he have written for the school magazine, or belonged to the French or Latin clubs, or something else that isn't too taxing?"

"You're a sharp one," Mr. Beasley said. "That's exactly what a lot of Crewe people thought. He's bright enough. Me, I always wondered if Merrill didn't enjoy poor health. And maybe traded on it a little."

"Well"—Cherry sighed—"rheumatic fever is a serious disease."

She asked Mr. Beasley what he could tell her about the Albee brothers at the present time.

"I'd judge Richard to be about twenty-five or six by now, and Merrill around thirty. Still in poor health. The two of 'em still live with their mother in that big white house of theirs—the father is dead. Wait a minute. I heard Richard's out of town, heard it about six months ago. Haven't seen him around for six or seven months."

Cherry pricked up her ears. "Do you know why he left?"

"No. Nothing special, or I would've heard. Everybody in town would've heard. Nothing unusual or alarming happened, I mean."

So far as the town knows, Cherry thought. A secret could be well guarded. The park attendant had no other recent news of the Albees.

"Can you tell me anything about the business owned by the Albee family?"

He could tell her only that the Albee factory was located just outside of Crewe. He "guessed" that Merrill operated it—"or maybe I should say he used to. Seems to me that factory is closed down."

"Are you sure? When did it close?"

"Well, I'm not so sure, at that. Haven't passed by on that road recently. But I heard something about the business having its troubles. Failing, maybe."

Cherry decided she had better visit the Albees. If the firm had closed down, that fact might be related to Richard's breakdown. Perhaps, though, it would be wise to visit one or two more impersonal sources before she ventured into the thick of a family and business situation.

"Well, Mr. Beasley, I certainly do thank you for giving me this information."

"Glad to be of help, ma'am." They solemnly shook hands. Cherry was walking back to Gwen's car when the park attendant called after her, "Hey! You didn't tell me why you wanted to know about the Albee boys!"

She smiled and climbed into Gwen's car. There wasn't time to explain. Besides, as Richard's nurse, she was pledged to keep his secrets.

~~~~~~

CHAPTER X

Mr. Steele's Story

IT WAS HALF PAST TWELVE BY THE TIME CHERRY DROVE from Gull Point back to town. In Crewe she parked the car on the main street, had a bite of lunch, and located the police station. She talked with a uniformed police sergeant in a bleak office.

The interview did not yield Cherry anything she did not already know from the telegram that the Crewe police had sent to Hilton Hospital. She was discouraged and asked a few questions.

Yes, the Albee business was still in operation; Merrill Albee ran it. Apparently Sam Beasley had been mistaken. No, the Crewe police had not made a special search for Richard because his brother, Merrill, advised them that Richard had left to work out some kind of personal trouble.

"He showed us Richard's good-bye note to back up his statement," the police sergeant said.

A good-bye note! This was news! If she could see what was in the note—But the police did not have it.

"As I remember, Merrill figured it meant," the police sergeant said, "Richard would return home when he had straightened out his affairs. He was upset about something. Something personal, it sounded like."

Upset about Susan? About his family? Cherry asked whether he knew how the Albee family members got along together. The sergeant looked back at her with cool, amused eyes.

"The police don't know about people's private relationships, miss. It's none of our business. No, I haven't heard of any quarrel, and Merrill sounded perfectly friendly about his brother. The best I can do is furnish you with the Albees' home and business addresses."

Cherry thanked the officer for his trouble and left. In the car she mused about what to do next. The good-bye note was a very interesting discovery. Possibly Merrill or Mrs. Albee had kept it, and might let her see it. Still she felt a reluctance to enter that white house and wade into some sort of complex or troubled situation. If she prepared herself with more facts—

What about visiting the Crewe bank where Mrs. Albee had an account? The bank officials might be able to tell her something about old residents like the Albees, and about the business as well.

Mr. Steele was a gray-haired, flinty-faced man behind a desk. He reminded Cherry of the mathematics teacher who failed her in algebra (she had deserved it). She started out on this interview gingerly.

"I've come to you, Mr. Steele, on behalf of a member of the Albee family." She showed her hospital credentials. "Do you know the Albees, sir?"

"Yes, I've known the family well through business for many years, particularly when Justin Albee was alive. A very pleasant association. I still sometimes see Merrill."

"Do the Albees have personal or business accounts here at the First City Bank, Mr. Steele?"

The bank officer looked startled but answered, "Mrs. Albee and Richard maintain personal checking accounts here. May I ask the purpose of your questions, Miss Ames?"

"One of our patients at Hilton Hospital is a young man who says he is—who may be—Richard Albee."

"Well! Indeed! That is exceedingly interesting! What's *he* doing in Illinois? And what an odd way you put it—'may be Richard Albee.'"

Cherry fidgeted in her chair. She had aroused the banker's interest, but his attitude toward Richard was so hostile, so suspicious, that she was alarmed.

"Mr. Steele, this young man is seriously ill. That's why there is some doubt about his identity, although we have reason to believe he *is* Richard Albee." She was trying not to reveal the fact of his amnesia. "If he weren't so ill and in need of help—I'm his nurse—I wouldn't have traveled all this distance. My visit to you is an effort to get help for a very sick and unfortunate man."

The banker listened to this guardedly. "How extraordinary. A nurse doesn't generally undertake—Well,

I am sorry to learn that Richard is so ill, and I will cooperate with you. You understand, however, that I do so out of feelings of loyalty for the Albee family."

For the family. Not for Richard. Why was he hostile toward Richard? All Cherry could do was to ask questions, feeling her way as she went along.

"Are Richard and Merrill in business together?"

"They were, until Richard suddenly went away. They might or might not be again, when Richard returns. I—ah—gather the brothers have not been on the best of terms recently."

"Over a business matter?" Cherry asked. "Or a family misunderstanding?"

Mr. Steele declined to disclose the exact cause of their rift.

"Does it involve their mother?" Cherry persisted. "I'm sorry to press, but this information has a bearing on Richard's recovery."

"I don't see how," the banker said rather testily. "Their mother? Both sons have always treated Mrs. Albee with the utmost consideration. I must tell you, Miss Ames, that Olivia Albee is in uncertain health."

So the mother was not well! This was no figment of Richard's imagination, either; this was fact. Cherry recalled how worriedly and guiltily Richard had talked about his mother, even, at first, believing her dead. Yet the brothers' rift was not about her. About what, then? She pressed the bank officer to tell her.

He hesitated. "I can tell you this much. Merrill won't be glad to see Richard again in any hurry, not after

what Richard did recently. Merrill has complained to
me about Richard—with justification, anyone would
admit. . . . Yes, about a business matter. . . . Well, yes,
it rather involves Mrs. Albee, too."

After what Richard did recently. Cherry recalled
her patient's feelings of self-blame. Was he actually
guilty of some wrongdoing? Getting information out of
Mr. Steele was difficult.

"You seem to have a higher opinion of Merrill than of
Richard, Mr. Steele," Cherry prompted him.

"Certainly. The older brother is more responsible,
more practical, has the cooler head."

"I can see how important that would be in running
the Albee business."

Mention of the business brought the banker to safer
ground; he was willing to talk freely on this subject. The
father, he said, had founded this business where medicines were developed and manufactured, and bulit it into a
well paying business. The Albee family had originated and
owned a formula for a "miracle drug" product that other
manufacturers and druggists needed and purchased from
them. Justin Albee had been careful to keep the exclusive rights to the formula in family hands. He had resisted
efforts of larger firms to buy out the business or to effect a
merger. He had, as planned, familiarized Merrill and Richard with the business, and left it to both sons as partners.

"Mr. Albee died about four years ago?" Cherry said,
recalling the Crewe police report.

"Yes. He was ill for seven or eight years. Bedridden.
Merrill left college—it was a sacrifice on his part, he left

without graduating—in order to operate the business during Mr. Albee's illness. As the elder son—he's four years older than Richard—Merrill was the logical one to take charge. In my opinion, Merrill has done a very capable job for so young a man."

"And Richard?" Cherry asked.

Mr. Steele's eyebrows went up. "Since we're talking candidly—I don't consider Richard much of a businessman. He remained in college all during the years Merrill operated the business alone. I understand Richard is a brilliant student of chemistry and biochemistry, so I suppose his many years of training were not wasted."

Mr. Steele told Cherry that Richard had shown a special talent in college for research in the so-called miracle drugs. He proved so adept that he was deferred from army service: that is, he was exempted except in case of war, and remained on call as a potential government scientist. ("So that's why," Cherry thought, "his fingerprints aren't on file with any of the armed forces.") Mr. Steele said that Richard did advanced, postgraduate studies and research until he was twenty-five, about a year ago. Then he entered the family business.

"He's twenty-six now?" Cherry asked. "How long was he active in the family business?"

"About six months. Quite long enough."

"But a research chemist of Richard's caliber—I should think that in a business that manufactures drugs and medicines, he'd prove of outstanding value."

"Perhaps. I don't know enough of the organic sciences to say. Merrill feels, and I am inclined to agree, that it's a pity Richard ever entered the family business at all. At least Richard left the financial and management aspects to Merrill—fortunately."

Why, *fortunately?* Cherry wondered. Was Richard a brilliant theoretical biochemist without a trace of practical judgment?

Mr. Steele was saying that since Merrill had already been in charge of the financial and management end, he did not welcome any interference by his younger, inexperienced brother. Richard for his part was glad enough to be left free to manage the production end of the business. He worked with a long-time employee, Mitch Johnson, the plant manager, in the six months before he went away.

"And why did Richard go away?" Cherry asked.

"You might say he absconded with twenty-five thousand dollars of this bank's funds."

Cherry almost fell out of her chair, and her voice died in her throat. When she recovered her composure and could speak again, she asked for details. Her patient a swindler? A thief?

"What Richard did," Mr. Steele told her, staring past her, "was to borrow twenty-five thousand dollars from us on his personal note. He said it was for use in the family business. Since Richard was just starting to earn a living, he had no personal collateral to offer, but he agreed to a claim by us on his share of the business, in case he could not meet his note. We scarcely thought a member of the Albee family would default," Mr. Steele said dryly. "When the promissory note fell due after three months, Richard disappeared."

"Disappeared," Cherry murmured, "or broke down."

"Disappeared, Miss Ames. Absconded. So far he has not made any repayment. He has not even had the decency to communicate with us."

How could a man without a memory communicate with the bank? Or had he lost his memory as a way of covering up a crime? Cherry was so distressed she could hardly think what to say or ask next, except to cling fast to one principle: the welfare of the patient, guilty or not guilty, was always a nurse's first concern.

"What happens to Richard next? Tell me, Mr. Steele, has the bank taken any action against him?"

The bank officer smiled faintly. "How could we, when we didn't know where he was? The bank trustees are discussing court action and placing a lien on Richard's share of the business."

That meant, Cherry knew, that Richard would lose his share, and that the Albee business would then be partly owned by the bank.

Mr. Steele continued, "We have taken other factors into consideration—so far. One is that any legal action against Richard would be extremely hard on his mother—might nearly kill her, in fact. The Albees are old clients here, old friends. Aside from the lien which we could claim on Richard's share of the business, Merrill has assured us he will see that Richard eventually pays us back, with interest. So far the bank trustees have waited, not very willingly. We hoped Richard would return and do the right thing. Now you tell me Richard is in the hospital!"

"Yes, he is, and he is a very sick man."

"Bah! He's found a convenient excuse! I suggest to you, Miss Ames, that Richard Albee fled to escape repaying his loan and is now pretending illness to escape lien action. What hospital did you say you're from? Hilton, Illinois, isn't it? I shall wire at once to your hospital authorities and to the Hilton police, and demand that Richard Albee be handed over to the Crewe police."

"No! Mr. Steele, you mustn't do that! He's not pretending—the doctors on the case will vouch for that. He was brought to us in bad shape—a motorist found him lying beside the highway—he's better after several weeks but he still can't—can't cope with this difficult loan situation."

Cherry doubted Dr. Hope would pronounce him recovered enough to deal with such a crisis. Poor young man! Yet *had* he used the business as a blind and deliberately tricked the bank out of twenty-five thousand dollars, then fled? If so, why had he been found six months later in rags? What lay behind these contradictions?

Look for motives, Cherry told herself. What did Richard want the twenty-five thousand dollars for? For his own use, one could argue, for once he obtained the money, he disappeared. But, in fairness, suppose Richard really had taken the loan for business purposes, then had lost his memory and wandered away. It was possible: everything Cherry had observed about Richard suggested he was a conscientious man.

Suppose he were not simply a thief, but a man at the verge of breakdown—suppose he *had* validly taken out a business loan. Then why could not the business repay? That was usual.

"Mr. Steele, why can't the business repay? That is, why can't Merrill repay on Richard's behalf? Aren't the brothers business partners?"

"Merrill has no responsibility for Richard's note. Merrill is in the clear. Richard alone took the loan. He took a *personal* loan. The note carries his signature alone."

What a burden! Cherry wondered whether this loan falling due had burdened Richard to the point of triggering his amnesia. It could have. If only she knew whether he had acted in good faith with the bank, or if he were guilty of theft! *Why* had he needed the loan? What circumstances had he been facing? It was essential for Dr. Hope to know.

Cherry did know one thing. Flight from memory has more, and deeper causes, than a single event like this loan. That is, there was surely more to Richard's story than the loan.

"Well, Miss Ames? I've answered your questions, but you haven't answered mine." Cherry came out of her thoughts with a start. "You haven't yet told me why Richard shouldn't be remanded to the police. He's not mortally ill, is he?"

Cherry sighed. She did owe Mr. Steele and the bank an answer. Although she was duty bound to keep her patient's secrets, she was just as obligated to act in her patient's best interests. If she remained silent and Richard were placed under arrest, at this stage of his recovery—

"All right, Mr. Steele, but I must have your word that you'll keep this information in strict confidence."

He looked doubtful, but nodded. Then Cherry told him that Richard Albee suffered from amnesia. She described his symptoms. The bank officer looked stunned.

"Richard is not faking, Mr. Steele. He has had a real breakdown. Under these circumstances, there is no point in arresting and prosecuting him now. Don't you agree?"

"Yes. I am so sorry."

"Do you think, in the interests of his making a recovery, that the bank might grant an extension of time on his promissory note?"

"I think so. I will recommend it to the trustees. Miss Ames, do the Albee family's doctor and lawyer know what has happened to Richard? Can't they help?"

"I plan to see Merrill," said Cherry, "and tell him about his brother. Mrs. Albee, too, if you think so." Mr. Steele nodded. "Then they can decide what steps they wish to take. But I don't believe Dr. Hope will release Richard, or even let him be disturbed, until he is better."

"I can understand that. I'll do what I can."

"Thank you very much, Mr. Steele."

Cherry asked the bank officer a final question. Did he know of any friend of the Albee family named Susan? Cherry had brought with her the letter signed "S." She showed it to Mr. Steele.

"That might be Susan Stiles," he said. "Judging from its tone and content, it probably is. She's an exceedingly nice girl, more a friend of Merrill's than Richard's, I believe."

Susan and her father, Dr. Stiles, used to live in Crewe. A few years ago, they moved to New York City. In the past year Mr. Steele had occasionally seen Susan and Merrill together in Crewe restaurants. He suggested that Cherry could locate Susan by looking up her father, Dr. George Stiles, in the New York City telephone directory.

"Mr. Steele," said Cherry, rising, "thank you very much. You've been a great help to Richard."

From a telephone booth in downtown Crewe, Cherry called the Albee plant. A secretary informed her that Mr. Merrill Albee was there but he was too busy to see anyone today. Cherry stated her name, profession, and hospital affiliation, and said she would like an appointment to see Mr. Albee about his brother, Richard, "with whom I have been in touch." There was a long pause, while the secretary apparently consulted Merrill. Then the secretary returned to the telephone and said, "Mr. Albee will see you tomorrow morning at eleven, Miss Ames. At the plant."

"Eleven. At the plant. Thank you." Cherry hung up.

It was too bad she had to wait until tomorrow. Perhaps she could see Mrs. Olivia Albee today. She could try.

The Albees' white house, on the corner of a broad avenue, was a big, pillared place, surrounded by hedges and trees. Cherry rang the doorbell and was answered by an elderly housemaid. Cherry introduced herself and asked whether Mrs. Albee was at home to visitors.

"Mrs. Albee is out," the maid said pleasantly. "I believe she has gone to the doctor's, and won't be home until dinnertime."

"I see—thanks—" Cherry was discouraged. It was half past three in the afternoon.

"Is there any message, miss?" the maid asked.

"No, I guess not. I'll try again."

Two hours later Cherry was back in New York City. At the Greenwich Village apartment, the Spencer Club nurses were busy preparing dinner. Bertha handed Cherry a bowl of potatoes to peel.

"I'll do it as soon as I make a phone call," Cherry said. "Where are the telephone books?"

"On the floor of Mai Lee's closet. She stands on them to reach the top shelf."

Cherry thumbed through the Manhattan directory, found a number for Dr. George Stiles, and dialed it. Someone who sounded like a housekeeper answered. Dr. Stiles and his daughter had just gone out, and would be out all evening with friends.

"When can I reach them tomorrow?" Cherry asked. "Any time in the afternoon," was the reply. Cherry left her name, said thank you, and hung up.

After dinner, which Cherry joined in in a preoccu-
pied way, she made another telephone call. This one
was to Dr. Hope, at his home in Hilton. She gave him
a detailed report.

"Good," said Dr. Hope. "Very good. But there's surely
more. Keep at it."

CHAPTER XI

The Patched Letter

MERRILL ALBEE WAS A DIFFICULT MAN. FIRST OFF HE
hinted to Cherry that she had inconvenienced him
in his morning's work at the plant. Then he said he
supposed the interruption was unavoidable, since he
did want news of Richard.

Cherry stifled a retort, and took a long look at Richard's brother. Merrill Albee seemed older than his age,
which was thirty; he was already growing bald. He was
a tall, thin man, with a pale, intelligent, angular face
that in no way resembled Richard's. His manner made
him seem older than he was, for he had that not-to-be-
questioned air of a business head accustomed to issu-
ing orders. This interview, here in his private office,
was not going to be easy. Cherry planned to come right
to the point about her patient, but Merrill Albee said:

"Excuse me, Miss Ames." He consulted his wristwatch, took two pills from a container in his pocket,

and swallowed them. "Can't always manage to take these on time," he muttered half to himself.

"Yes, the timing is important. I'm a nurse, as you know, Mr. Albee. Those look like tablets to counteract secondary anemia."

"They are." Merrill glanced at her with a first ray of interest. "I'm obliged to take an array of medicines and vitamins. A great nuisance."

Although she had some idea of his physical condition, Cherry tactfully inquired after his health.

"Oh, I've been in wretched health for years. Secondary anemia, arthritis, a damaged heart." Merrill Albee smiled bitterly. "It's an old story. My younger brother ruined my health for me when we were boys, in an accident in the Sound."

Cherry concealed her feelings. Merrill went on to say that Richard hadn't meant any harm, but that he, Merrill, nevertheless had suffered and, according to his doctor, would continue to suffer.

"That *is* hard, Mr. Albee." It was not her place to reason or argue with him. Apparently Merrill had convinced himself that Richard was guilty.

The secretary came to the door. "Excuse me, Mr. Albee, but the two suppliers' salesmen whom you asked to call are here."

"I can't see them today. I'm not feeling well today, and I already have enough to do. The men will have to call again."

"But they came all the way from New York, Mr. Albee."

"Please don't argue with me, Miss Gardner." The secretary stood there uncertainly, then left. "Now, Miss Ames, you have some news of my brother?"

"Yes, I am here as your brother's nurse, Mr. Albee. He is a patient at Hilton Hospital in Hilton, Illinois." She had planned to soften the blow, but Merrill showed no alarm. "Richard is an amnesia case."

"He—What? I don't believe it."

Cherry said patiently, "Your brother has lost his memory. When a motorist found him, our hospital ambulance brought him to the hospital with a broken leg. He was dazed and malnourished and in rags. We believe he had been wandering for several months. He didn't even remember his name."

Merrill stared at her, shocked and shaken. "How is he now? How long has he been at the hospital?"

"Richard has been under medical and psychiatric treatment for about a month. He's much better now."

Merrill reached for a denicotinized cigarette. "Then his condition can't have been too serious. I'm glad to hear he is better, and of course I want to do whatever I can."

Cherry wanted to shake this cold fish of a man. "Richard's condition was and is serious, Mr. Albee. He has not recovered by any means."

"Well, ship him home and our family doctor will look after him," Merrill said casually. Then he gave Cherry an anxious look. "What has he been doing for the past seven months, Miss Ames? Do you know? He walked out on me, and never had the consideration—even for our mother—to write or telephone home."

"He couldn't! He lost his sense of identity. He's forgotten what you and your mother look like."

"Amazing. But never mind that, for the moment. What has Richard been *doing?*"

Why was Merrill so anxious to know this? Cherry repeated that Richard had been wandering. "The psychiatrist wonders whether Richard broke down in Crewe, because of some trouble, and at that point started to wander."

"Oh, ridiculous. I was the last person to see Richard before he left, and he was perfectly all right. He *intended* to go away. Didn't that possibility ever occur to you hospital people?"

Cherry let the surface sarcasm pass. She was not here to quarrel, but to understand. She was concerned with the *reasons* for Merrill's hostility and scoffing. Under the circumstances, his lack of alarm was extraordinary.

"I'm going to show you something, Miss Ames, which will prove I am right."

Yes, *Merrill needed to be always in the right*, Cherry thought, remembering the park attendant's story, *and needed to prove Richard always wrong.*

From his wallet Merrill Albee took a tattered, folded paper and handed it to her. She smoothed it out gently, for the letter had been torn into small pieces and then patched together with Scotch tape. She recognized Richard's neat, scientist's handwriting. She had seen a sample of his handwriting when he had written a letter for one of her ward patients. The characters here were large and sprawling as if he had written in agitation.

"Merrill—I'm so ashamed of what I have done that I'd like to go away and never come back. I don't know how I can ever face Mother again. Tell her whatever you think best. I'll be in touch with you whenever I am able to make restitution, the fates willing. Good-bye—Richard."

Merrill said triumphantly, "There! You see? A good-bye note proves Richard intended to go away."

Cherry was not so sure. Perhaps Richard had deliberately intended to go away—or perhaps the letter was the despairing outburst of a man on the verge of breakdown. At any rate, to wander away with a blank memory was quite a different matter. What made her wonder was the fact that the note had been torn up, then patched together again. She asked Merrill about the patching.

"That means nothing," he said. "The message is there, isn't it?"

That was not the point. The point was to discover the circumstances under which Richard had written this note—and then torn it up?

Cherry knew that just prior to the onset of amnesia, her patient must have gone through a period of great emotional strain. On the edge of breakdown, in a black mood, Richard could have written the note. But he could also have had another stormy change of mood, a change of mind and heart, torn the letter into pieces after the relief of writing it, and thrown it away.

Then did Richard himself patch the pieces together? Cherry found it hard to believe that. It would be simpler to write another note.

Had Merrill found the pieces of the note and patched them together? Certainly, a good-bye note would have relieved Merrill from feeling too much concern about his brother's going off in the face of the loan trouble.

"Mr. Albee, did you patch the pieces of the note together?"

"Young lady, you're here to ask questions about Richard, not about myself."

"I'm sorry, Mr. Albee, but you see, it's necessary to know whether Richard ever discussed with you any plan to go away—apart from his letter."

"No, he didn't, but doesn't his letter of good-bye make his intentions plain and simple enough?"

Cherry forbore to answer. Merrill did not want to understand. "After you found the note, Mr. Albee, what search, if any, did you make to locate your brother?"

"You assume, Miss Ames, that a search was necessary. Here"—he took the letter back from her—"we have Richard's statement that he wanted to leave and, I believe, never wanted to return. Why, then, should I search for him? Why not let him alone? I felt it would be kinder to let him live his own life as he sees fit. And as I told you, he was—or he seemed to be—perfectly well when I last saw him, perfectly able to take care of himself."

"Yes." Either Richard's moment of breakdown did not occur in Merrill's presence, or Merrill did not recognize the symptoms.

"Would *you* search for a brother who leaves a good-bye note, Miss Ames?"

"*Yes, I would,*" she thought. "*I wouldn't let Charlie just disappear. Especially if he left a good-bye note written in such a heartbreaking tone.*"

It sounded to Cherry as if Merrill was not eager to find his brother. As if Merrill did not want to assume any responsibility for him and his bank loan.

"Mr. Albee, I realize you had no way of knowing that Richard was about to lose his memory. Now you do know, and if you could see him, you'd know what a rough time he has been through."

Merrill refused to be touched. "I am very sorry for Richard, but I don't see what you expect me to do— except, as I said, bring him home at once."

Dr. Hope would not want that, not yet. Cherry steered the conversation to the family business. Merrill responded to this subject.

"It's remarkable, Miss Ames, how little I miss Richard in the business. Oh, of course, he was a help in his own way. I grant that he is a fine chemist." Even this remark rang with an undertone of envy. "Richard spent many, many years in college while *I* kept the business alive. *I* worked, while Richard remained a student, a child. No one considers that I sacrificed the opportunity to complete my own education. But I suppose I can congratulate myself on having a highly educated brother."

Envy. Grudges. Self-love. How many times this morning, Cherry wondered, had Merrill used his favorite word "*I*"?

Merrill mistook her attentive silence for sympathy. "You know, Miss Ames, Richard came into the business as an equal partner. But I feel he did not deserve to. His contribution of time—six months before he left!—and effort has not been anywhere near equal to mine. It scarcely is an equitable arrangement."

"How did it come about, Mr. Albee?"

"Through the terms of my father's will. That was not entirely fair, either. You see—"

Merrill revealed that Justin Albee had given him to understand that he, the elder son, and handicapped as an aftermath of a serious illness, would inherit the larger share of the business. "But Mother always was sentimental about Richard." Their mother had insisted that the father write into his will and business papers an arrangement giving the brothers an equal share in the business.

Merrill—and Richard, too—did not learn this until after Justin Albee died a few years ago. It came as an unpleasant surprise to Merrill. He resented the equal terms. He did not hide from Cherry his disappointment at losing his promised special privileges over the brother who had "injured" him.

"It's been hard for me, believe me, Miss Ames."

"Yes, I'm sure it has been." *"Mostly because you made it hard for yourself,"* she added silently.

As Merrill Albee talked, Cherry could see how his resentment of Richard had been building, all the time the two boys were growing up, and how it had reached an intense pitch over the equal terms of the partnership. Although Merrill stated once or twice that he was fond of Richard, Cherry thought he was scarcely Richard's friend. She began to distrust Merrill.

"I'm sure you can see my point of view, Miss Ames?"

"I'm trying to see both your and Richard's points of view, Mr. Albee."

He was dissatisfied with her reply. "Perhaps I should tell you that Richard recently has embarrassed me very seriously, and has placed our family business in jeopardy. He is involved in—ah—some misguided dealings with one of the banks we do business with."

Merrill Albee leaned forward, eager to rally her to his own side. "Richard really should have used better judgment. Ours is a family business, we originated a famous formula, and have exclusive rights to it. Many other pharmaceutical firms, and banks acting for them, wish to merge with us, in order to obtain the right to use our formula." The bank officer had said the same thing, so in this much, at least, he was telling her unbiased fact. "Now Richard, because of the mess he's made of the bank dealing, has placed us in a position where we may be forced into a merger. We'd lose control of our family business."

Cherry remembered that the park attendant had hinted the business might be failing, and the bank officer had mentioned the possibility of placing a lien or claim on Richard's third share of the business. And Merrill, fairly or not, blamed Richard for the danger of losing control of the business. This, as well as the overdue loan, must weigh on Richard.

"Now do you see why I blame Richard, Miss Ames?"

Cherry did not attempt to discuss with this emotionally twisted man whether or not Richard was guilty in the matter of the overdue loan. Merrill in their entire conversation had been subtly blaming Richard for everything, including his health. He would do so on the subject of the loan, too. Cherry therefore kept away from the dangerous topic of the loan. "I'll have to find another person to help me learn the facts about the loan and the business," she thought.

Should she ask Merrill about the name Susan? By now she felt too wary of Merrill to chance that.

"Yet Merrill may be in the right," she mused as he complained further, "and Richard may be in the wrong. There may be factors about the loan and business situation which justify Merrill's blaming his brother. Merrill may be entirely above reproach. He *has* been a steady person, he *has* kept the business going, and stayed by their mother—whatever his motives may be."

But whether Richard was guilty or innocent, she must unearth the truth. Only in this way could Dr. Hope and she, too, help their patient to get well and face his life situation. Discovering the truth meant talking to more people.

"Mr. Albee, it would be a great help if I could talk to your mother."

"No, I don't want that." He quickly corrected himself. "My mother isn't well, and she must not be upset in any way."

"I understand. Has your mother been in poor health for very long? How serious is it, Mr. Albee—if you don't mind my taking an interest?"

Merrill said in some detail that it was learned, after a biopsy was made, that Mrs. Albee had a nonmalignant tumor that needed removal. The Albees' doctor had advised them that the need for an operation was not immediate, not an emergency—contrary to what Richard in his troubled state believed—but the need was serious enough.

"We found out she needed an operation just before Richard went away. Since he left, Mother has been so upset that she refuses to undergo the operation. Our doctor agreed to defer it. No, Richard doesn't know that. I think Richard did know there might be a lack of funds for the operation, thanks to this loan fiasco. An operation and convalescent care are expensive."

So his mother's health, too, weighed on Richard! Overdue loan—business in danger of being lost—his mother needing an operation—and Richard assumed it to be all his fault! It was enough to make anyone break down—*if true.*

"I must see your mother, Mr. Albee." He started to object again, but Cherry stood firm. "Surely your mother is entitled to news about her missing son. It probably upsets her more not to know, and imagine all sorts of horrors. Telling her where and how Richard is would set her mind at ease, don't you see? In the long run it would aid her health."

"No, I can't let you bother her. I'll tell Mother myself about Richard."

Would he? Even if he did, what partial or twisted version would he tell their mother?

"Mr. Albee, it is my duty, as Richard's nurse, to talk with his mother. If you won't let me see your mother,

I will ask the Crewe police department to give her the news of Richard."

He turned ashen, furious at being crossed.

"All right. All right. I'll tell my mother to expect you at our house tomorrow morning at eleven. I think that will be convenient for her. I'll prepare her for your visit."

"In his own strange and unhappy way," Cherry thought. Poor man. As a nurse she recognized that a person of inferior health and strength was often irritable, demanding, and had a chip on his shoulder.

"Thank you, Mr. Albee, and thank you for giving me so much of your time this morning. I'll come back to Crewe tomorrow."

He smiled mechanically, without enthusiasm, and had the secretary show her out of the plant.

"If Merrill's story is true," Cherry speculated as she drove back to New York, "then Richard is guilty of theft, or gross inefficiency, and of some irresponsibility toward his mother. But if Merrill's story is not entirely accurate, then Merrill—or circumstances—may be at fault in part, too. What a load it would lift from Richard if I could prove that! Well, my next step is to find out whatever their mother can tell me—and Susan Stiles, too."

~~~~~~

CHAPTER XII

Two Key Interviews

AT LAST, SUSAN!

When Cherry had driven back to New York City and telephoned Susan Stiles this afternoon, saying it was about Richard, she sounded relieved and invited Cherry to come over at once. So here she was in Dr. Stile's living room, aware that patients waited for him in his adjoining offices.

"I'll be brief," Cherry said. With a physician, and this friendly, concerned young woman, she felt free to discuss Richard's amnesia. Susan and her father were shocked to learn that he was ill. They inquired warmly about him.

"We don't know Richard or Mrs. Albee very well," Susan said, "though we're fond of them both, especially Richard. It's Merrill whom we know best—or rather, I do." Apparently Merrill was Susan's beau.

Dr. Stiles murmured something, which Cherry did not quite catch, about Merrill's being extremely critical of his brother, too critical.

"Why do you say that, Dr. Stiles?"

He was reluctant to talk about the Albees' personal relationships. So was Susan. As a doctor, though, and as a doctor's daughter, they understood why these facts were needed to help Richard's recovery. They stressed Richard's loyalty and devotion to his mother and brother. They told Cherry a little about the strain between Merrill and Richard.

Cherry produced the note signed "S," handed it to Susan, and asked, "Did you write this to Richard?" Susan nodded her pretty head. "Would you mind telling me what it means? Or what led you to write it?"

"Well, I—I hardly remember what I wrote in it." Susan accepted the note from Cherry and read it aloud. "'It was good of you to tell me what you did last evening. At the moment I didn't understand you. I hadn't realized he's'—that's Merrill—'under such a handicap. Now I do and I will make allowances. So don't worry.' Oh, now I recall what happened!"

Susan said that she had been a little impatient with Merrill over the small matter of his insisting on theater tickets for an inconvenient date, and she had unknowingly hurt his feelings. Richard had come to see her to smooth things out. He'd explained to her that Merrill, under the handicap of shaky health, never at ease or popular, was sometimes difficult—"but Richard insisted he's basically a fine person." He'd told Susan that she was the first girl Merrill had ever courted, and had asked her to be patient with him.

"I thought Richard was a darling to come and talk with me on Merrill's behalf," said Susan. "I was awfully touched by all the affection he has for his brother. I remember thinking 'It's almost as if Richard feels some special obligation to his brother—'"

Dr. Stiles was listening closely. He remarked to Cherry, "What my daughter and I cannot understand is why Merrill has been so little concerned that Richard suddenly went away, and sent no word home in several months. It's true Merrill felt a degree of concern. He mentioned some personal difficulty of Richard's—"

"Isn't it too bad Richard got into this terrible mess about the bank loan?" Susan blurted out. Her father looked disapproving. Cherry quickly said that Merrill and the bank officer had already discussed the loan with her.

"It isn't clear to me, though," said Cherry, "whether Richard really did a terrible thing, or simply a mistaken thing." She felt bound to defend him against Merrill's criticism of him to these friends.

"You see, Susan?" said Dr. Stiles. "I told you we had only Merrill's version of the story. Actually we don't know what Richard has done, or why he went away. We should suspend judgment, and take Merrill with a grain of salt."

"Well, I agree, Daddy," said Susan, "that Merrill's unconcern about Richard is pretty cold. I think we've been more worried about Richard than he has."

Cherry told them that it was important for her to learn from them about Merrill, as well as Richard, since the brothers' lives were closely linked. In the course of conversation it came out that Susan had been having frequent dates with Merrill for about a year now. He was courting her—lavishly. Too lavishly, Dr. Stiles said.

"Merrill has offered my daughter several expensive presents which she is not willing to accept. His presents are entirely too much, coming from a man Susan is not sure she wants to marry."

Susan gave a shaky laugh. "The more I refuse, the more hurt Merrill feels and the more he redoubles his efforts. I wish he'd stop spending so much money on me. It's embarrassing."

"Sounds really lavish," Cherry said.

"It's ostentatious, that's what it is. When we go out, it's always to the most elaborate restaurants and night clubs. I've told Merrill that I could be just as happy with something simpler, but he—he seems to be trying so hard to please me. He even bought one of those luxurious foreign cars, and explained it was to take me driving." Susan shook her head. "I don't mean to be unappreciative, but it's like living on whipped cream. Just too much richness."

Her father frowned at Susan's lack of reserve, but she said, "No, I'm even going to tell Miss Ames about the engagement ring. Either we tell her the facts or we don't, isn't that right, Daddy?"

Some months ago Merrill had bought Susan a very beautiful, very expensive diamond engagement ring, but she still had not accepted it. She was unsure of what she thought and felt about Merrill. Dr. Stiles remarked that Susan was right to have her doubts.

"It's as if—" Dr. Stiles started. "Let's say the lavishness of his courtship—Merrill's very first courtship—suggests that he is unsure of himself. It looks almost as if Merrill is trying to buy my daughter's affections. It's the only explanation I can think of. We went to the Albees' house to a party last year, and while they live very comfortably, it's not on the lavish scale Merrill offers Susan."

Cherry wondered what Richard and Mrs. Albee thought of Merrill's extreme generosity to Susan—or whether they were even aware of it. She hoped Dr. Stiles and Susan were not wondering what she was wondering—whether Merrill, in his frantic efforts to win Susan, could afford such presents, entertaining, and display. Cherry thought of the park attendant's remark that the Albee business might be failing. She thought of Merrill's ambiguous remark about a possible lack of funds for their mother's operation. Short of funds. … Yet, according to Susan, Merrill's lavishness continued right up into the present.

Was this heavy expenditure for Susan what the brothers were on poor terms about, just before Richard went away?

And if it was Merrill who had been spending heavily, why was it *Richard* who took out the loan—ostensibly for the business? Cherry wondered what the business books would show.

Or had Merrill been paying for Susan's entertainment out of some personal funds that he might have saved or inherited?

"I have no right to discuss with the Stileses this very private business of the Albee family," Cherry thought.

She stood up to go. "Thank you both ever so much. I'm going to see Mrs. Albee tomorrow."

"That's fine," said Dr. Stiles, and Susan smiled. "I think news of Richard will help her. In my opinion, Mrs. Albee is as much worried as ill."

A surprise was waiting for Cherry at the Spencer Club's apartment that evening—an airmail letter from Dr. Hope, propped up on the mantel.

The psychiatrist wrote, briefly, that their patient had been asking where Miss Cherry was and suspected she was contacting his family. Richard was upset at any prospect of a reunion.

"Reuniting Richard with his family," Dr. Hope wrote, "will be hard to effect. It probably will prove hard for everyone involved. A reunion may not even be possible or desirable. At the moment we can't foresee an answer to this. Much will depend on what information you bring back from Crewe."

Cherry could only hope that things would work out for Richard and his family. Her visit to Mrs. Albee tomorrow loomed up more urgent than ever.

Olivia Albee received Cherry in her upstairs sitting room. In appearance she reminded Cherry of her son, Richard, slender and dignified. She seemed to be a gentle, intelligent woman, firm in a quiet way. Cherry could see she was not well from the slow way she moved, but she held herself erect and smiled.

"I'm so happy to have news of Richard."

"Richard sends you his love, Mrs. Albee." Cherry felt it was all right to tell this fib, out of kindness. "I'm Richard's nurse, and Mr. Merrill probably told you—"

"He told me a little." The mother's voice trembled. "Exactly what is wrong with my son Richard? Please don't feel you must spare me."

"I'll tell you the truth, Mrs. Albee." And Cherry did, gradually, and with tact, stressing Richard's progress toward recovery.

Mrs. Albee, though saddened by the news of his amnesia, said, "How grateful I am that Richard is in good hands at your hospital! It's a relief to know, at last, where he is and how he is. You can't imagine how helpless one feels—*is*—when a member of one's family disappears."

Mrs. Albee had wanted to institute a search for Richard. "But I could not ask for statewide alarms, because Richard was well when I last saw him and able to take care of himself."

"Really well?" Cherry asked cautiously.

Olivia Albee reflected. "Not quite like himself. He was very quiet, and thin, and nervous. I knew he was overworked. When he suddenly went off, I didn't know what to think. Then Merrill showed me Richard's letter of good-bye and gave me to understand that Richard left voluntarily—had deserted us, in a way, and did not wish us to find him."

Yes, that was what Merrill wanted to believe, but was it true? Evidently Mrs. Albee had wondered, too, for she said:

"I did ask Richard's friends for news of him. Everyone was very kind, but our efforts came to nothing." Mrs. Albee's appeal to the Crewe police was not taken too seriously, in view of the good-bye note and Merrill's statements.

Mrs. Albee wanted to hear in detail all about Richard. Cherry softened the harsh parts, and described how much Richard was liked by the other men on the ward, and how bravely he was working to get well. Olivia Albee smiled, and touched her eyes with a handkerchief.

"How could I have been so blind not to perceive that he was under a great strain? I should not have simply taken Merrill's word for so much, either. I've come to realize, Miss Ames, that Merrill keeps me in ignorance about Richard"—she hesitated—"and about other matters. Merrill insists it's to 'spare' me—and that is so unnecessary."

In her relief at finally having news, Olivia Albee talked freely to her son's nurse.

"My sons are always so considerate of me. They think I'm not aware of the tension existing between them. I suspect they've quarreled recently, Miss Ames." Cherry remembered Richard "making up a story" of two men quarreling bitterly in an office.

"As if I couldn't see," their mother went on, "the sad contrast between the two boys all the time they were growing up. Merrill has had a hard time. He's often been ill and in pain. He never was strong enough to take part in sports and school clubs. He *has* tried to be outgoing and likable—he's made pathetic efforts. But as a result of his poor health, and of—let's not hide facts, Miss Ames—of his rather self-centered nature—Merrill was never popular. And Richard had always been so very popular, and took part in and won school track meets and swimming meets—" Mrs. Albee sighed. "Perhaps if his brother Richard had not afforded such a contrast to him, Merrill might have had a happier time of it."

"How did Richard feel about this?" Cherry asked.

Mrs. Albee hesitated. "Merrill put quite a few demands on him. He sometimes ridiculed him, for a joke. Richard is good-natured, and he took it in stride. He would do anything in the world for Merrill."

It sounded to Cherry as if Richard was so loyal to his older brother that he never saw—or perhaps would not admit, even to himself—that Merrill was cold and envious.

"To me, of course," Mrs. Albee said, "each is infinitely dear in his own way. I do think Merrill has an easier time now that he is a grown man, and in charge of a business for several years—he feels more assured now."

Cherry said that in the course of visiting Crewe on Dr. Hope's instructions, she had met Merrill's friend, Susan Stiles, yesterday.

Mrs. Albee's face lit up. "Susan is a dear girl. She's good for Merrill. His first romance, and he is taking it with desperate seriousness. Too much so. So seriously that he has—" Mrs. Albee frowned and fell silent.

"May I ask why you say too seriously?" Cherry hoped to find out whether Mrs. Albee knew how lavish Merrill's courtship was—what large expenses it involved. She wondered if Richard had known.

"Perhaps I shouldn't say anything," Mrs. Albee said. "I don't really know how Merrill's romance is progressing, even after a year. Perhaps he is too self-conscious to tell me. And he doesn't know I've discovered—" Mrs. Albee shook her head. Half to herself she said, "I see him primping before his dates and looking ever so worried and earnest—like a young boy who is not sure of himself."

That was Dr. Stiles's comment, too. Cherry asked what it was Mrs. Albee had discovered. But the woman's eyes filled with tears and she would not answer.

Cherry did not press. Instead, she guided the conversation to the brothers' boyhoods. Mrs. Albee talked about the swimming mishap. "The 'accident,' or rather its aftermath, made quite a difference in his life, and naturally in Richard's, too."

"Mrs. Albee, I'm aware of Merrill's having contracted rheumatic fever," Cherry said. "Do you think that the unfortunate swimming episode was Richard's fault in any way?"

"No. It was entirely Merrill's own fault."

"Do you think, though, reasonable or not, that Richard blamed himself in any way? Or that Merrill blamed him?"

Mrs. Albee looked upset. "It's hard to say. What an odd question! I—I hope there was no blame."

"Forgive me, Mrs. Albee, but do you think that Richard's devotion to Merrill was due to pity because of Merrill's illness?"

"No. Richard has always loved his brother. Even before the illness, he was intensely loyal and affectionate toward his big brother."

And Merrill, in his shame at being outdone in so many respects by Richard, had not found it in his nature to respond to Richard's love. Cherry sighed. Mrs. Albee was trying to excuse Merrill.

"Although the illness was due to his own youthful lack of judgment, and *perhaps* Richard's too, Merrill has paid dearly for it." Their mother recalled how Mr. Albee had favored Merrill after his illness, feeling the delicate son needed more spending money, a car, extra consideration in view of his impaired heart. "Richard felt it was only fair. Not I. Their father meant to do the right thing, but in effect he only encouraged Merrill to be selfish," said Mrs. Albee. "Then the time came for Richard to graduate from Junior High School and enter Senior High School, where Merrill was a senior—Merrill had lost a year of schooling because of his illness, you see. I insisted the boys attend separate high schools. And later on I insisted that my husband give the boys *equal* shares in the business.

"I realize Merrill was disappointed—he had believed he was going to control the business. Considering Merrill's disappointment I've wondered how well the boys got along together in the business. In front of me, they put up a show of amity. But I noticed that they never told me much about the business, especially not Merrill. That is why I made inquiries, just recently, and that is how I discovered—" She was unable to go on.

"If you want to tell me about it, Mrs. Albee—" Cherry tried to encourage her to continue. "Does your discovery affect Richard?"

"Yes! Very much. Oh, it would be a relief to tell you, Miss Ames! I'm still stunned at what I learned. You see, I've discovered—almost by accident—a terrible state of affairs. I haven't told anyone about it—out of family loyalty—only our family lawyer knows—"

Mrs. Albee said that she, like the two sons, owned one-third share of the family business. But for the past year her returns from the business were much smaller than usual, and she was alarmed. Merrill was evasive about this, hinting that Richard disappeared because he may have dipped into company funds. Mrs. Albee simply did not believe Richard would behave in this way. Her repeated questions to Merrill only netted more evasions.

A few weeks ago Mrs. Albee consulted the family lawyer, and asked him to investigate. The lawyer sent an accountant to the plant, to examine the firm's books. The accountant reported that the books showed two astonishing facts. First, Merrill had been paying himself extra bonuses over the past year, without reporting them to Richard or his mother—apparently he had purchased the expensive foreign car, among other things, with these bonuses. Second, Merrill had charged the business for the presents he had given Susan—telling the bookkeeper the Tiffany bill was for several small presents for customers and their wives at Christmas, which was not true. He had also charged Susan's restaurant bills and theater tickets to the business as pretended "business expenses." As a result of these sizable shortages, the business was failing.

"And was this why," Cherry wondered to herself, "it was necessary to take out a loan? To save the business?"

Mrs. Albee said tiredly, "I've been too distressed about my discovery even to discuss it with Merrill. Though I'll have to, sooner or later—"

Cherry wondered if Richard knew Merrill had been taking funds? Had Richard discussed the matter with Merrill? If so, that would illuminate the recent trouble between the brothers. Cherry asked Mrs. Albee these things.

"I'm not sure," their mother replied, "whether Richard knew much or anything at all about the shortages. You see, when Richard came into the firm about a year ago, Merrill insisted that the business and financial angle was already his department, and the chemistry and production was more naturally Richard's department. Richard agreed to this arrangement—he took it for granted that his older brother, having been a long time with the firm, knew how to run the business. And Richard is first and last a scientist, not much interested in the business end. I believe that Merrill—he's something of an autocrat—even discouraged Richard from looking over the firm's books. Richard told me he was annoyed. But he's always been so loyal and devoted to Merrill, and of course he's always trusted his older brother."

Cherry asked, "You said something about your sons having quarreled, Mrs. Albee?"

"I'm afraid they quarreled often in the weeks just before Richard left. Merrill told me a little about an unfortunate loan Richard had taken out, or something of the sort." Evidently, Cherry noted, Mrs. Albee had been kept largely in ignorance about the loan, too. "Miss Ames? Did all of this lead to Richard's loss of memory?"

"It's possible it contributed, Mrs. Albee."

It occurred to Cherry that all during this loan trouble, Merrill must have been under his share of strain, and probably still was.

"About their quarrels, Mrs. Albee—?"

"Something finally came to a head, I don't know exactly what," Mrs. Albee said to Cherry. "All I know is, one day last April, Merrill came home exhausted and angry. He told me he'd had a terrible quarrel at the plant with Richard, and that Richard walked out and didn't come back. He—he brought me Richard's note of good-bye."

A terrible quarrel. … To Cherry, this news of a quarrel was medically important information. The quarrel might have been the final blow that, after weeks and months of strain, triggered Richard's amnesia. Dr. Hope had said that a mounting period of anxiety invariably precedes amnesia. Richard must have been terribly worried about the loan as the repayment date came nearer and nearer. What exactly was the emotional stress on her patient just before his breakdown? What had Merrill said to Richard during that final quarrel? For many years Merrill had resented Richard, and this stored-up resentment reached its peak last April. What had Merrill blamed him for, or threatened him with, on the day Richard disappeared?

Merrill would not tell her, and Mrs. Albee did not know. Richard knew, but could not remember.

Cherry looked discouragedly at Mrs. Albee, who sat up straighter in her chair.

"Miss Ames, it's done me so much good to unburden my mind to you! I've been silent and done nothing about this situation for too long. But now that I know where my son Richard is, and how he is, I feel I have the strength to act. I promise you, Miss Ames, and more important, I promise myself," Olivia Albee said with spirit, "that I will have Merrill make amends to Richard for this. I will insist that Merrill do the right thing in a business way, too."

Knowing how thorny Merrill was, it was easier said than done, Cherry thought.

"Miss Ames, I want to go to Hilton to see Richard and bring him home. ... No, no, I'm not so ill that I can't do it. Merrill would have to escort me, of course."

Cherry felt alarmed. She was sure her patient should not see Merrill, even with Mrs. Albee, while he was

still groping to find himself; the encounter would be
a shock. Richard might need preparation. Dr. Hope
would have to be consulted. Cherry explained as much
of this as was tactful, and said to Mrs. Albee:

"I'll have to consult Dr. Hope, and find out when you
and Merrill may come for Richard. The moment Dr.
Hope approves, I'll notify you."

"Thank you. May I send Richard something?"

Cherry smiled at Richard's mother. "I was thinking
of the same thing. Have you some familiar belonging
of Richard's which I could take back to him? To help
stimulate his recall?"

Mrs. Albee smiled, too, and thought. "I knitted a
blue sweater for him that he's fond of and has worn a
lot. Blue is his favorite color."

She asked the maid to find the sweater in Richard's
room, and gave it to Cherry. They said good-bye, then.

"I'll look forward to seeing you in Hilton, Miss Ames.
Soon, let us hope."

"Yes," said Cherry uncertainly. "Don't worry, Mrs.
Albee. What you've told me, and what I've managed to
learn on this trip East, ought to help Richard a great
deal."

She left the Albees' house, regretting that she had
not been able to find out just where the loan fit into
this troubled situation. Why, Cherry wondered, was
it taken out as a *personal* loan if it actually were for
business purposes? Why had Richard alone signed for
it? Mr. Steele had already told her all the Crewe bank
knew. Mrs. Albee knew very little about the loan. As for

Merrill, Cherry realized, Merrill would not be willing to tell her anything about this. Probably only Richard knew the whole story about the loan, if he could be helped to remember it.

That had to be the next step.

By the time Cherry drove back to New York City, and put Gwen's car in the garage, it was three thirty P.M. Her job in Crewe and New York was completed, and Cherry was eager to deliver her information to Dr. Hope and see her patient just as soon as possible. An afternoon plane? Why not? She would miss spending the evening with the Spencer Club, but she'd save half a day tomorrow. From a phone booth Cherry reached the airline she wanted, and was able to make a reservation for six P.M. That would give her enough time to pack, say a quick au revoir to any Spencer Club members who might be at home, and catch the bus to the airport.

The nurses' apartment was empty and quiet. Cherry saw a note on the mantel, in Josie's scrawl.

"Cherry—In case you come home ahead of us, we're all going to the theater this evening. Gwen's nicest patient gave us a flock of tickets. You're going, too—save the evening for us."

Before she left, Cherry wrote a note of her own and propped it on the mantel.

"Gwen, Mai Lee, Josie, Bertha—Awfully sorry but I'm going to Hilton, instead of to the theater with all of you. This case is urgent. Give my ticket to some worthy character. Best love to all of you, and hope the play will be a good one."

CHAPTER XIII

A Wall of Mist

CHERRY REPORTED BACK TO HILTON HOSPITAL FRIDAY morning, October tenth. She had been gone for four crowded days. Dr. Hope, whom she was eager to see at once, was not here yet, the head nurse said. The door to Richard's room stood open. That was a cheerful sign.

"Good morning, Richard!" Cherry rapped on the doorframe. "May I come in to say hello?"

"Miss Cherry! I missed you." The cast had been removed from his leg. "Dr. Watson cut off the cast—bivalved it, he said—yesterday." Richard's wide, friendly smile was a cheerful sign, too. He swung himself off the bed, using his crutches, and pulled up a chair for her. "Dr. Hope told me you were in Crewe visiting my family."

"Yes, and I brought you this."

Richard recognized the blue sweater. "I'm glad. It's an old friend. Mother knitted it for me." Richard

157

stroked the sweater. "How is my mother?" he asked rather anxiously.

"She's fairly well, and very happy to hear news of you, and she sends you her love."

Cherry was astonished at the good change in him. Earlier he had insisted his mother was dead. Now he was lucid, calm, and cheerful. But though she waited for him to say, "How is Merrill?" he did not. He eyed Cherry with an expression she could not fathom.

She thought, "I'd better be careful what I say to Richard. Who knows what's in his mind about my visit to Crewe?" She excused herself before Richard could question her, and went to Dr. Hope to discuss the situation.

He was just taking off his hat and coat. In the morning sunshine, with his bright fair hair and athlete's stance, Harry Hope looked vital enough to cure any patient.

"Well! Miss Cherry!" He pumped her hand. "Sit down and tell me all about it. Or, first I'll tell *you* some good news."

Their patient, he said, had made an unexpected spurt of progress in the last few days. Perhaps the knowledge that his nurse was paving his way with the family aided him. While Cherry was away, Richard recalled that his mother was alive, and that he felt responsible or guilty about her health in some way he didn't understand. He remembered for the first time that he had an older brother, Merrill, with whom he, a chemist, was a partner in the family business. Richard, Dr. Hope said, felt vaguely that he had wronged

Merrill, and that he was in some trouble involving Merrill. Richard also surprised Dr. Hope by remembering that the business was failing. He insisted that it was his fault, insisted he had somehow ruined the family business or its credit.

That was as far as Richard could remember, as far as he was able at present to face his predicament. Dr. Hope commented that it took courage and effort on Richard's part to come this close to the unbearable realities.

"I could hardly wait for you to come back with information," Dr. Hope admitted to Cherry. "Can you tell whether Richard's new recall is fact or fantasy?"

"Dr. Hope, no matter what Richard believes, he did not ruin the business. He did *not* injure Merrill, nor his mother."

And Cherry told the psychiatrist all that she had learned in Crewe and in New York.

"I see," he said, "I see. Richard's feelings of guilt and self-blame are no more than symptoms of his illness, then. Poor fellow. Well, let's decide how we'll use what you've learned."

Dr. Hope said they had two aims now—to relieve Richard's unnecessary feelings of self-blame, and to aid his recall.

"We mustn't tell Richard anything right out—only stimulate his recall. Our job is to help him recall by himself." He briefed her carefully. "One thing I don't understand, Miss Cherry. Why did Richard alone take out a *personal* loan for the business?"

"I couldn't find out, Dr. Hope. I suspect that's the heart of Richard's troubles."

That same Friday afternoon, with Dr. Hope present and watchful, Cherry described to Richard her visit with his mother and brother.

"Aren't they a nice family?" Richard responded. "I wish you could have met my late father. He was a fine man. He left my brother and me the business he founded, of course as equal partners."

Of course, Richard said, and said it calmly. So Richard was unaware that Merrill had always resented his having an equal partnership.

"You don't have much to say about Merrill," Dr. Hope prompted him.

Richard spoke loyally of his brother, but guiltily, too.

Cherry, guided and aided by Dr. Hope, slowly and with great care, reintroduced to Richard some of the facts she had learned in Crewe. She gave him hints. She reminded him of what he had recalled by himself, and urged him to recall a step further, then another step.

"You were on the beach near the big, jagged rocks, you and another boy. Could it have been you and Merrill?"

"Yes. Merrill and I went swimming. Racing. I mean, we swam far out—I never should have dared him—"

Frowning, fumbling for the half-drowned memory, Richard brought back the whole painful episode.

"It all started, in a way, because Merrill had a habit of teasing—well, taunting me. About how I couldn't measure up to him in some ways because I was younger and smaller and four years behind him in lots of ways. I never minded much because I was good-natured, I guess, and mostly because I sensed that Merrill needed to 'triumph' over me."

"That wasn't very kind of Merrill," Dr. Hope said.

"Well, that's how he was and I admired him so much that it didn't matter. Until one summer when he was fourteen and I was ten. It was a rather cool day—"

On that day the brothers had bicycled to the beach. There, in front of friends, Merrill made some sharp remarks to Richard and the little boy felt humiliated. In a burst of spirit—not malice—he had dared Merrill to swim far out with him, beyond the swimmers' area, to where they could race. Merrill accepted the dare to race.

What neither boy took into consideration, Richard said, was that Merrill had limited strength, which was not important so long as Merrill did not overstrain himself.

The swim took them far out. Merrill wanted so badly to win that he overexerted himself. Exhausted, he had trouble fighting the strong current. Richard saw this and attempted to help him. But Merrill in his pride— friends on the shore were watching—fought off Richard's aid. He told Richard, "Keep away!" and Richard, despite his concern and better judgment, did as his older brother insisted. People on shore started to swim out to help, but Merrill waved them back, too.

When the boys reached shore, Merrill argued with Richard as to who had won the race—a pointless, inconclusive argument. But during that time Merrill was exposed to a cold wind, and grew chilled. The hardier, younger Richard withstood the wind.

Then the boys bicycled home in their wet bathing suits, under jeans and sweatshirts. This further exertion and exposure also harmed Merrill.

When they reached home, Merrill was on the verge of collapse. Their mother went to the telephone to call the doctor at once. In the moments she was away, Merrill blamed Richard for "making me get sick." Richard was so distressed and abashed at seeing his adored older brother near collapse that the blame sank in, unreasonable as it was.

And later when Merrill was in the hospital, and still later during Merrill's long, grim convalescence at home, he blamed Richard again. The serious impairment to Merrill's heart was now evident. Merrill was fourteen; Richard was only ten; he could not outargue Merrill's claims that "you dared me"—"you *knew* I wasn't very strong"—"why didn't you help me in the water, no matter what I said? Couldn't you see I was exhausted?" Richard felt so badly at seeing Merrill ill, so guilty at having dared him and at not having helped him, that he humbly accepted the blame. Telling about it even now, Richard still had the old, guilty feeling. And still later on when Merrill was a semi-invalid, and Richard strong and active, the steady, silent looks of reproach from Merrill weighed on Richard.

Worse, Merrill made his charges secretly, never telling the parents and swearing little Richard to secrecy. He hinted morbidly that the parents would never forgive Richard if they knew "what you'd done to me."

"And you never told your mother or father about this?" Cherry said. "Why didn't you talk it over with your parents, Richard?"

"Because"—he was almost in tears—"Merrill warned me it might kill Mother if I told. It would upset her so badly. She was always in shaky health, a latent heart condition."

So Merrill had used the mother's health as an additional weapon over Richard. In careful phrases Dr. Hope gave Richard a hint of this.

"No, no, you mustn't blame Merrill," Richard said quickly. "Because in a way it *was* my fault that Merrill nearly drowned, and was half an invalid afterward. I've always felt I ruined Merrill's life. I owe it to him to help him in every way. He's never had much of a life. Nor many friends, except recently. There's a nice girl named Susan Stiles—"

So Richard had pleaded Merrill's cause with Susan as one more means of "making up" to him an injury Richard had never inflicted.

"See here, Richard," said Dr. Hope. "In exactly what way did you cause Merrill's ill health?"

"Well, I—It's hard to say exactly. Exposure—overexertion—my dare—Merrill *said* I did."

"No, Richard, that is not true."

Dr. Hope, and Cherry too, reasoned with him and endeavored to show him that the mishap was Merrill's own fault. They pointed out to him that he had carried around with him for years the mistaken ideas Merrill had implanted in him, under stress, at ten. Re-examine your ideas now, they urged. Stop thinking as if you were still ten years old. Gradually, with much work by all three of them, it dawned on Richard that he was blameless. After so many years of feeling guilty, he could scarcely believe it.

"It is true," he said wonderingly. "It's as if a load has been lifted off me."

"And can you still believe your parents would have blamed you? Weren't they fair-minded and loving with you?"

"Yes. Oh, yes, yes!"

Dr. Hope and Cherry gave him encouragement and moral support ("supportive therapy," Dr. Hope called it). They pretty much convinced him. Richard was greatly relieved, and much happier.

"To think I've been behaving as if I were still a scared child!" he exclaimed, laughing a little.

Best of all, Richard said his feeling of "strangeness" was gone. He remembered smoothly now, as if there'd never been anything wrong. He remained a little hazy about events of just last year, but "it'll clear up." He was confident he would recapture the rest of his lost memory soon.

"I think you will," said Dr. Hope, smiling.

The three of them were elated and hopeful. Richard was nearly well! Just a little further to go—

On Saturday and Sunday, which was Columbus Day, Cherry rested at home. Her mind was nearly at ease about Richard. Their patient, at the psychiatrist's recommendation, was relaxing this weekend, too. They were going to try for another big effort on Monday.

Monday afternoon Dr. Hope, Richard, and Cherry started on what they told one another would be the final step of the recall. Dr. Hope asked whether Richard could recall anything about having difficulties with Merrill in the business. He did not risk mentioning the loan that hung over Richard's head.

"Trouble with Merrill at the plant?" Richard concentrated, staring at his hands, trying to remember. "That's right. We quarreled. We—It's a terrible thing to say, but I remember I half believed Merrill was helping himself to company funds."

Now they were getting somewhere!

"Here again we mustn't be too harsh toward Merrill," said Richard hastily. "For the first time in his life he'd fallen in love. With an awfully nice girl, Susan Stiles. You know he's—well, awkward in getting along with people. He just doesn't know how to be a suitor. For that reason he'd offered Susan some presents, and I suppose he needed a few extra dollars."

A *few* extra dollars! To Cherry it was evident that Richard never guessed the full extent of what Merrill was spending in order to appear more attractive to his girl. So Richard was still excusing Merrill, still taking all the blame on himself, still had the old feeling of guilt toward Merrill. Last Friday's talk had not entirely eradicated it.

"I did what I could, in spite of doubts," Richard said apologetically, "to encourage my brother in his new role of suitor. I tried to help Susan see what a good person he is. But after a time—" Richard got up, took his crutches, and restlessly moved around the room. "I began to wonder. It was the ring that set off my doubts, I think. Merrill was dressing one evening and I happened to come into his room—"

The diamond engagement ring! It sparkled on Merrill's dresser, and Richard admitted its size, beauty, and value stunned him. He had looked at the name on the jeweler's box—one of the most expensive shops in New York. Merrill must have spent a fortune for it! Where had he gotten the money? From the business, was the only answer Richard could arrive at. Especially since the business was mysteriously failing.

Next day, Richard recalled, he asked Merrill to let him see the books. Merrill refused and quarreled with him. "Can't you trust your own brother?" Merrill had demanded. "Don't you trust my business judgment?" Yet Merrill told Richard repeatedly that the business was failing.

Richard grew more worried. He managed to see the books, which showed he had invested the loan in the business, and "I wondered why a loan taken out for the business had helped for only a short time."

Cherry started. This was Richard's first mention of the loan.

Richard sat down on the bed and let his crutches fall to the floor, with a crash.

"Go on," Dr. Hope said mildly.

"I can't."

"Yes, you can."

Richard swallowed hard and his voice came out thin. "To my astonishment I learned from the books that Merrill had been paying himself extra bonuses—large ones. He'd never told Mother or me about his extra bonuses. And all during last year he charged Susan's gifts to the business." Richard suddenly stopped speaking.

Dr. Hope prompted him. "And you challenged Merrill with these facts?"

Richard pressed both hands to his head. "Headache. All of a sudden. A blinding headache." He was pale and sweating.

Dr. Hope sighed and watched their patient. One minute ticked past, two minutes, three minutes. No one spoke or moved. Then Dr. Hope gestured to Cherry to try once more.

She leaned forward, speaking gently to Richard. "When I was in New York I learned some facts from Mr. Steele—at the Crewe bank. Do you remember him?" Richard's eyes were like stones. "Doesn't the name Steele recall anything to you?"

"No." Richard sat there blank, silent. He looked ill. "I can remember and see certain places and people. But there's a wall of mist rising up between them and me."

He had reached an impasse, just when they were making great and final progress.

Dr. Hope got up with a look of defeat. He said gently, "All right, fellow," with a pat on Richard's shoulder, and walked out. Cherry said a few words to Richard and followed.

She found the psychiatrist in the office, slumped in a chair. He made no effort to hide his discouragement.

"I'm nonplused," he said to Cherry. "I'm just not able to penetrate deeply enough into the patient's feelings. Have we overlooked some important aspect of the case? What have I done wrong?"

"Perhaps you didn't do anything wrong, Doctor," said Cherry. "Perhaps you've gone as far in one direction as anybody can go. Now the wall of mist presents fresh problems."

He looked at her gratefully. "That's right, we have to find another path, in order to break through. My techniques are inadequate at this point. I must find a new way. But what?"

Next day, after Richard had a long sleep, and ward recreation, Dr. Hope and Cherry tried again. "Doesn't the name Steele bring back something that happened? Something important?" Simply telling Richard the facts would not put them back into his memory; that is, would not solve his reasons for flight from memory. "Imagine the plant, imagine you're in Merrill's office— what are you talking about?"

But Richard could not remember. Even with the aid of a new drug, next day, it was impossible to break through. He grew difficult and depressed.

"We'll have to abandon the interviews and questioning," Dr. Hope told Cherry. "If we don't, we may push Richard back to where he was four or five weeks ago."

By Thursday Dr. Hope had devised a plan. He instructed Cherry to draw up, with the patient's help, his life chart. This was to list chronologically all the main events of Richard's life, with dates. The gaps where Richard's recall failed would show the trouble spots in his life. The big, stubborn gap was recent: the loan.

"What I hope will happen," said the psychiatrist, "is that in making this chart, Richard will recall everything at once, in one sweep. It could come suddenly."

Cherry and Richard started right to work. Richard was rather listless and hopeless, and Cherry had to keep after him. Together they wrote out a sort of diary, in snatches, and patched these into a chronological pattern. An account of most of Richard's life history emerged after two or three days' work. The gaps troubled Richard. Cherry could have filled in several of them with what she had learned in Crewe—except for two key events: why Richard alone took out the loan, and what had happened during the final quarrel between Richard and Merrill. She was as puzzled as Richard himself.

Dr. Hope studied the life chart over the weekend and then discussed it privately with Cherry. From this nearly complete information he pointed out how Richard's amnesia came about: Richard was trapped in an impossible situation and, unable to cope, blacked out mentally.

Much would depend on how Richard's reunion with his family went, especially with Merrill. If the encounter was unfortunate, Richard might lose the ground he had gained and become ill again—probably in some other form than amnesia.

To arm Richard for this family encounter, Dr. Hope and Cherry tried various approaches to help Richard recall the gaps. He made pathetic efforts, saying, "Maybe I'm just tired." He actually attempted to relieve Dr. Hope's concern by pretending to be cheerful. As his memory faded out, he grew sleepless, and more depressed.

The three of them put in a bad week. Then Cherry had an idea.

On Friday afternoon, October twenty-fourth, after six weeks of treatment, Cherry took Richard for a long-promised drive into the country. She had Dr. Hope's permission and she had borrowed her father's car. The day was raw and windy, with leaves blowing off the trees and clouds scudding across a dull sky. The weather did not matter, Cherry's purpose did.

"I wish I could drive," said Richard. Though the cast was off, he still needed crutches. The leg was stiff, but physical therapy treatments were helping to correct that condition. "I love to drive. Riding alone with you is fun, nearly as good. Where are we going?"

"Just to admire the autumn foliage," Cherry said. "And one stop."

She drove Richard through quiet, peaceful country roads to the old church and graveyard. It was here, not far from the highway, where Richard had said he "came to consciousness" and tried to think who he was.

Cherry stopped the car. They sat quietly, listening to the wind rattle the dry leaves and watching birds wheel high around the church steeple.

"I remember this place," said Richard.

"Can you remember what you thought, then? Take your time. Easy does it. We're in no hurry."

Richard gazed out across the churchyard and autumn fields. For a long time he made a lonely effort.

"No. Nothing comes back, Miss Cherry."

"Then we'll just drive and enjoy ourselves. Don't be disappointed." She hid her own disappointment.

For the next half hour Cherry drove Richard through the country roads. She offered a little, light-hearted conversation about Hilton, and the picnics and barn dances she'd enjoyed around here. She watched Richard relax in body and mind.

Then an extraordinary thing happened. They were driving up a long, steep hill, and they could feel the exhilarating power of the car as it carried them up, up. Near the crest Cherry smoothly shifted gears—and it was as if the gear wheels in Richard's mind engaged, too. He suddenly shouted, "I've got it! I remember everything now! My memory is running as smoothly as this car!" They shot out onto the crest of the hill. "I've reached the top of my own hill!"

It was true. Everything in Richard's mind had slipped into place. Almost all of his memory had returned. He spilled over with part of his memories to Cherry on the drive back to Hilton—they could not get back fast enough!—and he told the rest of it to Dr. Hope and Cherry at the hospital.

What Richard remembered, clearly and easily, was this:

Richard had learned from Merrill that the business was failing. This troubled Richard on its own account, and because their mother needed an expensive operation. As Richard understood or rather misunderstood it, the operation should not be deferred too long. Merrill told Richard it was necessary, if they were to save the business and their mother, to secure a large bank loan in a great hurry. He instructed Richard to sign a three-month promissory note, and Merrill promised to sign the note also.

Richard obtained the loan from the Crewe bank, but Merrill never signed it. Merrill was out of town that day on business and phoned in: "Don't delay, put the loan through. We must have the money today to meet bills and the payroll." Richard, trusting him, became solely responsible to pay back the loan.

The Crewe bank paid the money to Richard as a personal loan. He deposited the sum in his personal account at the Crewe bank, or more exactly, the bank paid the loan directly into his personal account. Then Richard put this money into the business. The company books showed this investment.

Merrill advised Richard not to tell their mother about the loan nor anything of business matters while she was ill. Richard agreed. He left business and financial arrangements to Merrill as usual, and went on about his own production work.

Just before the promissory note fell due, Richard asked Merrill for company funds to pay it back. Merrill showed him the books: the business was still failing.

Richard knew, to some extent, that Merrill had been spending much money on courting Susan Stiles. Now he wondered whether Merrill got the money by dipping into company funds. Richard had never had access to the books, but now he asked questions. He and Merrill quarreled.

In their final quarrel at the plant, Richard told Merrill he now understood where Merrill got the funds for the diamond engagement ring and the luxury car, and why the business was failing, and why their mother's operation was deferred. Merrill angrily denied everything. They had a terrible scene.

In a self-righteous rage Merrill pointed out to Richard that Richard alone was responsible for the loan note. He threatened to tell their mother that Richard had ruined the business because he was unable to repay the loan. He accused Richard of ruining not only his own personal credit but damaging the business's credit as well. None of these things were true, but Merrill convinced him. He told Richard to get out, and stay out, rather than inflict further injury on the business and their mother.

Richard faced an impossible situation. He must pay back the loan within a very few days, but could not. If, to repay, he assigned his third of the business to the bank, exclusive ownership of their original share formula would pass out of the Albee family's hands. The business was failing. There were no funds for his mother's operation; a charity ward was the only alternative. To sell the entire business was to abandon all that Justin Albee had built up. His brother had ordered him out of the business, and would turn his mother against him.

In despair Richard wrote a good-bye note, scrawled in haste—then tore it up and threw it away. He scarcely knew what he was doing.

He walked out of the plant a pauper, deep in personal debt, jobless, perhaps homeless. Under such stress, Richard lost his memory. This was last April. ...

Driven by anxiety, he kept on the move. With a small amount of money in his pocket, he boarded an inter-state bus that took him into the region of Hilton. That was as far as his money would take him. Then he hitch-hiked. He lived by doing odd jobs, sometimes on farms. As summer ended, he remained in and around Hilton picking up odd jobs where they were more plentiful. During parts of his six months of wandering, Richard's memory had been and was still spotty. He still could not remember how he broke his leg or how he hap-pened to be on the highway where a passing motorist had found him.

"Don't worry if you can't remember quite every-thing," Dr. Hope said to Richard. "You are cured, but a cure almost never brings *total* recall. Certain small incidents will always be lost."

Richard smiled and sighed. "I'm tired."

Cherry smiled at him. "Of course you are. Look at all you've relived, in telling us your whole story."

"I propose three cheers for Richard," said Dr. Hope. "In fact, for all of us!"

Now it would be possible, Dr. Hope said to Cherry in private conference, to attempt a reunion between Rich-ard and his family. It would be hard. Richard had more confidence now, but he still could be easily shaken. He would have to come to terms of some sort with Merrill—and he still must find a way out of the loan difficulty, with or without Merrill's help.

Cherry hoped that Olivia Albee—and, if necessary, Dr. Hope—would be able to prevail upon Merrill to help Richard repay the loan. The business, if properly managed, could probably repay it: it had always been a prosperous business until Merrill started withdrawing funds for his personal use. She knew Dr. Hope to be as anxious as herself about how the family reunion would go, and its far-reaching effects upon their patient.

Late that Friday afternoon Cherry had the hospital Social Service Department wire Mrs. Albee that she and Merrill could come now. Within half an hour Mrs. Albee replied by telegram: "We are coming at once. Will arrive tomorrow."

Cherry went back to Richard's room and told him the news:

"My family here—tomorrow? Mother and Merrill—I'm afraid they have faded or grown distorted in my memory. I can't imagine how it will be to see them again!"

CHAPTER XIV

The Final Step

RICHARD WAS UP ON CRUTCHES AND DRESSED, WEARING his blue sweater, on Saturday afternoon. That morning the visiting chaplain had spent a half hour with him, soothing him and lending him courage to face his family. When Richard had thanked the chaplain for his kindness, Cherry heard the chaplain reply: "Remember that we love you here."

Now she and Dr. Hope were waiting with Richard, in the last few minutes before his mother and brother were due to arrive. Richard looked around his little room.

"This is where you put me back together, almost piece by piece. I'll be homesick for this hospital."

"Come back to say hello sometimes," said Cherry.

"And see that you stay all in one piece now," Dr. Hope said with a grin.

"I will," Richard answered them both. "As soon as I can afford to, I'm going to send bathrobes to all the fellows on the ward. Mrs. Peters wrote down their sizes."

The orderly came to the door and said Richard's visitors were in the office on this floor, with Dr. Watson. Richard stood up tensely, then sat down again. Cherry touched his hand. Dr. Hope said, "Please bring them in, George," and stared out the window, which he didn't generally do.

Dr. Watson did not come in with them. Olivia Albee entered first, physically shaky but her eyes alight, eager to see Richard. She seemed a little apprehensive but determined. Richard sat perfectly still on the bed, looking at her.

Then Merrill Albee followed his mother in, and Cherry was struck by the change in the man. For one thing, the subdued way he followed his mother in showed that Mrs. Albee was now in command of the situation. Merrill looked drawn and chastened, as if he had done a great deal of soul searching. Merrill must know his loan fiasco was out in the open now.

The three Albees hesitated. In these first instances of confrontation, Dr. Hope and Cherry hung back. Richard stared at Mrs. Albee, then at Merrill, back to Mrs. Albee, as if they were strangers. His mother said, wanting but hesitating to move toward him:

"Oh, Richard, I'm so happy to see you!"

"I'm happy to see you, too," he said politely. His face cleared. "Mother, you can't imagine how I've missed you. Are you all right?"

He swung himself up on his crutches and rapidly went over to embrace her. He forced a smile for his brother.

"I've thought a lot about you, too, Merrill."

Merrill nodded, and avoided meeting Richard's gaze. He muttered something about "Mother ought to sit down." Cherry came forward then, to greet the Albees and introduce Dr. Hope. Richard pulled up a chair for his mother. They all sat down, uneasily.

It was Dr. Hope who did most of the talking. Mrs. Albee's eyes never left Richard's face; she was clearly appalled at what her son had suffered. Dr. Hope reassured her, while Merrill listened but never offered a word. Merrill's mouth was tightly closed and his angular figure stiff as a ramrod.

Dr. Hope turned to him, not genial for once. "Well, sir, how do you think your brother looks?"

"Not bad, except for the leg, and that's mending. If you hospital people think I'm responsible for Richard's wandering off—"

"You're entirely blameless, eh?" Dr. Hope challenged him. "You're not your brother's keeper, is that it?"

Cherry noticed Richard start to sweat. He could still be upset by Merrill.

"We're all our brothers' keepers," Mrs. Albee said. "We have to be."

"I suppose that's true, Mother," said Merrill, "but Richard has some responsibility, too, for his own actions. He isn't a child. If you're thinking of the loan—"

Cherry felt Richard's eyes upon her, silently asking her for support.

Dr. Hope said dryly, "I wasn't thinking of the loan. But since it's on your mind, let's talk about it."

Merrill shifted in his chair, nettled. "If you insist. It's all quite simple. Richard signed for the loan, and he alone is responsible for it. Perhaps I do have some—ah—moral obligation to help him out—this is an awful mess we've all gotten ourselves into. But I refuse to be blamed for Richard's erratic actions, wandering off like a tramp—disgracing us—"

Richard shook his head in denial.

Dr. Hope was about to speak when Olivia Albee said firmly, "You agreed with me, Merrill, that you are morally responsible, in large part, for what has happened to Richard. Don't forget that."

"Oh, I'll help him, all right. But you can't expect me, as head of the firm for many years, to—"

"I do expect you to help Richard repay," said Mrs. Albee.

"Very well. I don't deny my arrangement—ah—voting myself bonuses—was wrong. A mistake on my part." Merrill's self-righteousness was wavering.

"Mr. Albee, wasn't the loan affair a mistake, too?" Dr. Hope asked. "Can you tell us why you didn't sign the note along with Richard as you promised?"

Richard looked immeasurably anxious. Merrill's plain face tightened.

"I did intend to be a cosigner with Richard. It just happened that I was delayed in New York that day on business, and the firm couldn't wait for funds. That's the truth."

Dr. Hope nodded, giving him the benefit of the doubt. "And once Richard had assumed the responsibility—?"

"Then I thought 'Why not leave it that way? It's fair enough. I've put in many years of work here at the plant while Richard remained in school. And he comes in as a full partner! Now let him contribute something more, too.'"

Merrill admitted that when Richard went away, it seemed like a stroke of luck for himself. He had always daydreamed of having sole control of the business, and now was his chance. He found and patched together Richard's good-bye note, quieting his conscience with it. Richard could take care of himself.

"And now that you see your brother in the hospital, do you still feel that way, Mr. Albee?" Merrill uncomfortably pressed his lips together. "See here, Mr. Albee, as a practitioner I can assure you that your brother has really been ill. Now, no illness, no handicap, is a disgrace. But as your mother said, we all need one another's help. None of us lives alone, Mr. Albee. None of us gets sick alone, nor gets well alone."

"I'll—I'll help Richard. I realize I've gotten myself into an awful mess. You may not believe it, any of you, but I *have* been trying to straighten things out since Richard left. Do you think it's pleasant to have such a situation on my conscience?"

Richard said almost shyly, "It sounds as if you've been straightening out your thinking."

For the first time the two brothers looked full at each other.

"If you mean remorse," Merrill said, "yes. You've been on my mind. On my conscience. Way back, too. Maybe I—We never got along as well as we should have, and I—It wasn't your fault, Richard."

"Mr. Albee," Dr. Hope said quietly, "why don't we all forget old wrongs and old resentments? For Richard's peace of mind, and for your own."

The room was very still. "I—I'd like to, Doctor. I've been unhappy for years about these feelings. You may have the right answer." Merrill turned again to his brother sitting on the bed. "Maybe you were right, too, to study for so long. Maybe your being a first-rate chemist is the best thing for the business."

It was an enormous admission. Richard said, "It's all right. Forget it." Mrs. Albee reached over and touched Merrill's thin arm. He looked away, shamed.

"It's a relief to have all this out in the open, finally," Merrill said.

There was an awkward pause. Richard asked, "How's Susan?"

"She's fine, thanks. She knows some of our—my mess." Merrill turned to Cherry with an odd half-smile. "You talked to her, too, didn't you? You know, at first I resented your visit but I don't now. Your visit forced me to look at the unvarnished truth. The way I'd been excusing myself for years. I've had a bad conscience, Richard, about using so much of your loan money for

Susan's ring. And Susan wouldn't even accept it. That's an irony."

Mrs. Albee said, "I think Susan will care more for you, now that you won't stress material things so much, and now that you'll be kinder to Richard."

They talked a little about how to repay the loan. Merrill, very much shaken, promised to make restitution personally, out of his salary as partner, for the sums he had taken from the business.

"But if I'm to be able to do that, Richard, I'll need your cooperation in running the business."

"I'll be on the job Monday morning," Richard said. He looked toward Dr. Hope for permission.

Dr. Hope nodded and smiled. "You'll be there."

Cherry accompanied Richard as he walked through the ward saying good-bye to Tommy, who was allowed out of his wheelchair now, and to the fracture patient who had triumphantly discarded his braces, and to the spine patient for whose birthday two volunteers were bringing in a huge cake with candles, for the entire ward. Good-bye to Mrs. Peters, the head nurse, to Ruth, to George, and a special good-bye and thanks to Dr. Watson beaming in the doorway.

Dr. Hope and Cherry went downstairs with the Albees to the hospital's main floor. A taxi was waiting to take them to the airport.

"How can we thank you?" said Mrs. Albee.

Merrill knew how: he wrote out a check for Hilton Hospital to pay for Richard's care, and promised to send a second check for a contribution as soon as he could afford it.

Richard held on tight to Cherry's hand. "Lean closer." He whispered in her ear, "You're the best nurse and best friend any patient could ask for."

Then he got into the taxi with his family. Dr. Hope and Cherry stood a moment longer on the steps, in the cool wind.

"Patient cured," Dr. Hope said. "Case closed."

"I'm so glad." Cherry and Dr. Hope looked at each other with mutual admiration. Cherry said, "I certainly learned a great deal by working with you, Dr. Hope. I never before nursed a case like Richard's."

"You did all right." Dr. Hope smiled at her and added, "That's the understatement of the year. You're an excellent nurse. Let's go in. Your other patients and Mrs. Peters will be glad to have you back on the ward full time."

In case you missed *Cherry Ames, Boarding School Nurse*...

CHAPTER I

Lisette

CHERRY WISHED THE TRAIN WOULD GO FASTER. SHE was still out of breath from running for it. She pressed her cheek against the window to admire the green fields and fertile farms through which the local train poked along. Cherry's mother, who knew the headmistress of the Jamestown School for Girls from their own school days, had warned her that the school was deep in the country. Fortunately, it was not too far from Hilton, Illinois, which meant that she would be able to spend all school holiday vacations at home.

As the boarding school nurse, she would have full charge of the school infirmary. It would be fun to work with young people and a refreshing change from her last job—an unexpectedly thrilling assignment as nurse to a country doctor—something new, something different. If there was anything Cherry enjoyed, it was meeting new people. She was glad that she was a nurse because nursing, in its many branches, provided an *Open sesame* to new and exciting experiences—and because more importantly, a nurse can help to alleviate human suffering. She remembered what her twin brother Charlie had said jokingly when he put her on this train in Hilton:

"Don't set this boarding school on its ear. Wherever you go, twin, you make things happen, but you bring doggoned good nursing too."

It gave Cherry a good, warm feeling to know that her pilot brother, and her parents, too, were proud of her. They had made that clear during this past week, when they'd had such a satisfying family reunion, in their big, old-fashioned house. The week's rest had left Cherry's cheeks glowing rose-red and her black eyes sparkling. Even her jet-black curls shone with extra good health. She felt fully ready to tackle her new job.

She stood up, slim and tall, to stretch for a moment and noticed again the girl at the other end of the car. Only about fourteen years old, and small for her age, she was absorbed in a thick volume which lay open on her knees. The girl leafed through several pages, then as if finding what she sought, read eagerly—leafed, read, searched again. She read, Cherry thought idly, as if that book held all the answers to all her questions—whatever they were.

When the train pulled into Jamestown, Cherry noticed that the girl was getting off, too. They were the only two passengers who alighted. Jamestown consisted of a crossroads and a few stores, sheltered by magnificent oak trees. Only a few farmers, driving in for supplies, were outdoors in the heat of the afternoon. Cherry looked around for a station wagon or other car from the school, half expecting to be met. Hadn't Mrs. Harrison received her telegram? Perhaps she should telephone the school. Then Cherry spied a sedan with a sign in its windshield: *Taxi*.

But the young girl from the train was already making arrangements with the taxi driver. Cherry heard her say:

"—to the school, the Jamestown School."

Cherry approached them uncertainly. This was probably the one and only taxi in town, and in the country people often shared rides.

"I beg your pardon, but I'm going to the school, too, and since there's no school car here, I wonder—"

"Please share the taxi with me," the girl said at once and pleasantly.

So they stepped in and settled back. The driver started off through leafy tunnels formed by the arching oaks. Cherry and the young girl did not speak for several minutes. It was one of those ripe, golden afternoons when it feels as if summer will last forever, yet the school term would begin within a few days. Cherry was arriving early in order to get the infirmary in good shape, but what was a student doing here so early, she wondered.

Cherry glanced at the girl who had drawn away into her own corner of the seat. She was slight and pale, with a cloud of dark hair falling onto her shoulders.

"Since we're both going to the school," Cherry offered, "we might introduce ourselves. I'm Cherry Ames."

The girl smiled. "I'm Lisette Gauthier." She was rather shy. "Is this your first time at the school?"

"Yes, it is. Yours, too?"

"Yes, Miss Ames." The girl glanced away, hugging the big book to her. She seemed to be struggling with shyness, then overcame it in a rush. "I came to the school a week early, you know." She did not say why. "I went into Riverton to do some errands, and to visit the library. It's bigger than the school library."

"What an eager student!" Cherry exclaimed. "Studying before the term even begins."

"Oh—no—I mean, yes. It isn't exactly studying." Lisette did not reveal what the thick book was. After that, the girl sat quiet and guarded in her corner.

The taxi drove on past gardens where the scent of flowers floated on the air. Cherry remarked on the delicious fragrance, and—to choose another safe conversational subject—she mentioned her contact with Mrs. Harrison, the headmistress and owner of the Jamestown School.

"I've never met Mrs. Harrison but her letters have been awfully nice," Cherry said. "I'm looking forward to meeting her this afternoon."

Lisette turned and this time her smile had real warmth. "Everyone loves Mrs. Harrison. You will, too, I know you will. She's—well, you'll see! Can you imagine anyone else who'd let me come to the chateau a week early, and who'd even—"

The girl broke off, as if she had been about to say too much. Cherry filled the embarrassed silence with a cheerful remark about the fun of starting a new term, especially at a new school. Lisette looked at her with gratitude. Her eyes were ebony black and seemed to fill her ivory face. A funny little sprite, Cherry thought, first too shy to talk, then talking *almost* too much ...

All of a sudden the taxi slowed, and the driver, grumbling, coasted the car to the side of the road and hopped out for a look at the motor. He poked and examined and then went to peer in the gas tank.

"But the gas gauge reads better'n half full," he muttered.

Cherry glanced at it. So it did.

"Gauge isn't workin'," the driver said. "Gas tank is bone dry. I'll have to go for gas. A mile's walk in this broiling sun to the nearest gas station!"

He stamped off, carrying a metal container. The two girls were left alone together in the back seat of the sedan. Trees shaded them, but still it was going to be a long, warm wait.

"What wouldn't I give for a soda right now!" Cherry said. "Chocolate for you?"

"Chocolate for me," Lisette agreed. Her eyes danced like Cherry's own. She glanced at Cherry with obvious curiosity, although it was apparent that she would never intrude with questions. Cherry tried to ease things for her.

"You think I'm one of the new teachers, don't you?"

"Well, you look a little bit too young and too—"

"Too what?" Cherry laughed.

Lisette swallowed. "Too young and fun-loving."

"To tell you the truth, I'm to be the school nurse."

"Oh! That's nice. I've always sort of wanted to be a nurse."

"Lots of girls want to," Cherry replied. "A lot of them really do it, too."

"It's a sympathetic profession," Lisette said thoughtfully. "I always think of a nurse as a friend."

"Well, I hope you and I will be friends."

Lisette responded with such a glowing face that Cherry could not help but respond, too.

"I don't think," Lisette said very seriously, "that a few years' difference in our ages is important." She pretended to be busy adjusting the car window. "Do you?"

"Of course not."

Then Lisette was telling her, as fast as the words would tumble out, about her scholarship and her family and her wonderful luck in coming to the Jamestown School.

"All my life I've wanted to come here! And father always wanted me to attend boarding school. A really good one! I couldn't tell this to everybody, Miss Ames, but honestly, I'd never be here if it had been left up to my poor papa." She said *papa*, French fashion. "It's the greatest luck that I've a scholarship. Imagine. A year's scholarship and my room in the dormitory, everything, a regular guest!"

"It *is* wonderful," Cherry said. "I didn't know boarding schools gave scholarships."

"They don't very often. It's just that Mrs. Harrison is so generous. Not that she can afford—I mean—"

Lisette broke off short again.

Cherry's curiosity was aroused. How did the girl know what Mrs. Harrison could afford if she was a newcomer to the school? Then, too, what was she doing here a week early? Was it because of some family problem?

"What about your *papa?*" Cherry asked, since it was obvious that Lisette was trying to change the subject. "What a cunning way to say it!"

"We spoke French a good deal at home in St. Louis," Lisette said. "Especially Papa. He spoke beautiful French, although he was American-born. And he was a delightful host, and he knew dozens of funny stories, but that's about all Papa could do. He just wasn't a practical man. He tried hard to earn a living, but—My heavens, I *am* telling you a lot, Miss Ames."

"I'll respect your confidence." Cherry thought the girl must be starved for companionship, she seemed to be so glad to make a new friend. "By the way, wouldn't you rather call me Miss Cherry? It's friendlier."

Lisette looked pleased but suddenly shy again.

"You say your father *was* and *had,*" Cherry prompted.

"He died three years ago," Lisette told her.

"Forgive me. You must miss him very much."

"Yes, we do. It's hardest on Mother. For another reason, too. She's had to earn our living, you see—Papa only left us a tiny bit of insurance. And a collection of beautiful books of poetry," Lisette said wryly. "Mother says one can't be angry with a dreamer who simply couldn't cope with life. Papa did mean well." Lisette's voice trailed off.

"Is your mother in business?" Cherry asked.

"She gives music lessons."

No wonder Lisette was in need of a scholarship, Cherry thought. Teaching music was, as a rule, an uncertain way to make a small living.

Lisette was saying much the same thing, but in words chosen to save her pride. Her mother had made all of Lisette's dresses for the coming school year—it was less expensive than buying the dresses at a shop. Lisette hoped that her mother would come to visit her at the school, but she was busy with her pupils, and then there was the matter of fare. It was clear to Cherry that Mrs. Gauthier was making a sacrifice to send Lisette away to boarding school, even with the aid of a scholarship.

"I'm going to make this year count," Lisette told Cherry earnestly. "It's my big chance. I *must* make it count."

"I'm sure that you will," Cherry encouraged her. "Attending a fine school is a wonderful chance for any girl."

"No, no, you don't quite understand. It's something special for me! To come to *this* school, to the chateau, that's what I've always wanted."

Cherry wisely remained silent, touching the leaves which brushed the open car window. She knew from her nursing experience the importance of *not* asking questions. But she hoped that Lisette, of her own accord, would tell more. For Cherry sensed an unhappy situation here behind Lisette's carefully chosen phrases, and she would like to help her.

"Do you suppose our driver is *ever* coming back?"

"I forgot to tell you," Lisette said, "that the school station wagon is in the garage for repairs. Maybe we can beg a ride from the driver of that funny little wagon coming up the road."

"But she's heading away from the school," Cherry commented.

A plump, jolly little woman was driving the horse. She wore an old-fashioned sunbonnet; a wide straw hat rested on the horse's head, with holes for his ears to stick through. What captivated Cherry was the waves of flower scent from the wagon which held a few baskets of flowers. As the woman drew up alongside, she called:

"Whoa, Jupiter! Afternoon, young ladies! Is it hot enough for you?"

"We'll have cooler weather soon," Cherry answered. Lisette only managed to smile.

"You're from Mrs. Harrison's school, I'll wager. I'm Molly Miller from Rivers' Crossing—that's more of a crossroads than a village. Maybe you've heard of me and my flowers? I have a real nice nursery. Been out selling bouquets today."

"I've been admiring them," Cherry said, intoxicated with the rich scents. Most of the baskets were empty but in the remaining bouquets were a bewildering variety of blossoms.

"Mrs. Miller, I've been brought up right here in Illinois," Cherry said, "but I've never seen a home-grown bouquet with so many different kinds of flowers."

"Oh, we pride ourselves around here on our flowers." Molly Miller's weather-beaten face beamed. "Now, this is a specially nice bunch—so many varieties, four kinds of roses, night-scented stock, a few zinnias, asters—"

Abruptly, Lisette leaned across Cherry to inquire, "Are those for sale?"

"Why, certainly, young lady." Molly Miller named a small price. In her eagerness Lisette all but seized the bouquet from her. The farm wife looked pleased.

"Why don't you come over and see my garden and hothouses some day?" she invited them. "It's well worth a trip, if I do say so myself."

Cherry thanked the friendly woman, who gathered the reins tighter and clucked to her horse. As the wagon wheels started to turn, Lisette called out:

"Wait a moment—please! What's the name of this white spray—the one that smells both sweet and tangy? It's an odd scent—"

"Now, young lady," the farm wife called back, "I must hurry home. But you come and visit me—like I told you—" She waved good-by to them and the horse trotted merrily up the road.

Cherry waved back, then turned to Lisette, who was rapturously smelling the bouquet. She had never seen anyone enjoy flowers as much as Lisette.

"Miss Cherry, I didn't mean to—well, snatch the bouquet for myself, you know. I'd like very much to put them in the infirmary. Or at least half of them."

"For the empty beds to enjoy?" Cherry commented, hoping that there were no patients yet. "No, you keep the flowers, Lisette. Thanks, anyway."

"Look at the roses! White, fawn-colored, yellow, and those big red cabbage roses. Don't you love roses? What do you think this strange scent can be?"

Cherry and Lisette went through the bouquet, naming each flower. They were uncertain of one special rose, and unable to identify the silvery-white spray. Whether the odd, lovely odor came from flower or leaf of the silvery spray was a question, too.

Not until they heard gasoline gurgling into the taxi's tank did they notice that their driver was back, dusty and disgusted.

"I'd better git me one of Molly Miller's horses," he said, noticing the bouquet. "Sorry to keep you waitin'."

The taxi started off again. This time, they turned off the main highway and followed side roads. Birds sang on the boughs, a brook bubbled along.

Cherry sat up straighter, inquisitive to see where they were heading. She powdered her nose and straightened her hat, with one eye on the road. Presently she saw the tall, flat roof of a house, half hidden in trees but rising above them.

The taxi followed a gravel driveway which led into large, rather neglected grounds. Several smaller frame buildings stood among the grove of oak trees, but it was the main house which held Cherry's attention.

"It does resemble a chateau!" Cherry exclaimed. The lovely old building, surrounded by gardens, gave an impression of dignity, even stateliness. Its tall, narrow style was more Victorian than French, with arched windows and two small formal entrance porches, at front and side.

"Yes, folks around here used to call it the Chateau Larose," the driver said. He had appointed himself a sort of guide, as the three of them stood before the house, admiring it. "That's to say, they called it that when a private family resided here. Before the school started up in here. That's some years ago."

Cherry turned to Lisette, expecting some natural tie might exist between the girl with the French name and the house of a style transplanted from France. But Lisette remained silent, though a stroke of pink appeared in each ivory cheek.

"I must be mistaken," Cherry thought. "There are French descendants in St. Louis. The French founded the city—and it's in this general area. Perhaps Lisette wanted to see this chateau simply because it *is* French!"

The driver was waiting for his fare. Both girls opened their handbags and Lisette fumbled.

"I'm afraid I didn't bring enough. Or else spent too much—"

"Never mind," Cherry said. "I'll take care of it."

"Maybe I put my change in the inner pocket—" Lisette shook her purse, and as she did so, the bouquet and the heavy book on her arm dropped to the ground.

The book fell open. Cherry, who stooped to retrieve it, saw the book snatched away and snapped shut. She was a little surprised at Lisette's haste—as if she did not want Cherry to see what the book was about. Pretending not to notice Lisette's strange action, Cherry picked up the bouquet, then turned to the driver and took care of the fare.

"Thank you very much, Miss Cherry," Lisette said in a small voice. "I'm terribly embarrassed. I'll repay you."

"I'll be embarrassed if you do. I'll tell you what! You may contribute one red rose to the infirmary. Here are your flowers."

Lisette smiled shyly at her as if to say, "I like you." Then, as she stood silently before the house, the girl seemed to forget Cherry, seemed to be in a world of her own. Half to herself she murmured, "Papa and I always dreamed of this old house. Now I'm really here."

Cherry was puzzled. "And you came early to look around?" she said sympathetically.

Lisette turned crimson. She withdrew into herself again and did not reply. Cherry regretted that she had spoken so hastily, though she intended only a friendly interest! Why was Lisette so evasive and touchy?

"Let's go in the house," Cherry said, still puzzled. "I'd like to meet Mrs. Harrison. Will you introduce me?"

Lisette led the way into the house, which was cool and quiet. No one was in the entrance hall. Lisette knocked on the open door of an attractive reception room, and, since no one was there, went on into the huge sitting room which was Mrs. Harrison's office. The room was shaded, the walls were lined with books and photographs. At the desk a golden-haired woman sat writing.

Lisette said quickly, "Mrs. Harrison, here is Miss Cherry Ames," and then the girl vanished.

In case you missed *Cherry Ames, Department Store Nurse ...*

CHAPTER II

New Friends, Old Friends

CHERRY WOKE UP FRIDAY MORNING WITH A SLIGHT SENSE of dislocation. This must be No. 9, because hunched in the other twin bed she could see Gwen's familiar red hair and a curve of freckled cheek. Cherry had let herself in sleepily after midnight and found the apartment dark, all her fellow nurses asleep.

"I'll bet nobody even knows I'm here this morning," Cherry thought. She sat up and rubbed her eyes. In that case she could beat the others into the one bathroom and squeeze in a shower.

"Good morning, Cherry," Gwen yawned. "I see you're back again." She leaned over and whacked Cherry on the back. "Ha-ha! *Your* back again! Get it?"

Cherry groaned. "Please, not so early in the morning. How's your aunt? Did she stuff you with turkey?"

"We gobbled the gobbler!" When Cherry said *ouch*, Gwen struggled to a sitting position. "Don't blame me. It's that punny Betty Lane. I caught punitis from her."

Betty Lane was staying at No. 9 temporarily. She, too, had earned her R.N. at Spencer, but a year after Cherry and her friends had graduated. Therefore, Betty was only an honorary member of that august body, the Spencer Club. She was a pleasant girl, except for one thing, Cherry discovered—Betty had just beat her to the shower.

Cherry took one look at her wrist watch—she'd forgotten to turn it ahead an hour, upon returning east. Golly! No time for breakfast. She'd better hustle! Cherry washed in haste, practically jumped into her clothes, and called:

"Gwen? Ready to walk to the subway with me?"

"Gwen just left," Vivian called from one of the other small bedrooms. "That's what she gets for working way out on Long Island. Bertha said to tell you hello and good-bye."

"Mai Lee? ... Oh, she's visiting friends, isn't she?" Cherry pulled on her coat. " 'Bye, kids. See you at dinner."

The remaining two, rushing for their own jobs, called mumbled good-bys to her. "Well," Cherry thought, "I just hope the people at the department store aren't *all* in this scrambled state."

Cherry checked in at Thomas and Parke's a little earlier than the crowd of employees. She walked quickly across the main floor toward the bank of elevators. What a surprise! Yesterday while the store was closed, the display artists had transformed the main floor into a Christmas festival. Giant artificial snowflakes sparkled and spun slowly overhead, while fantastic cherubim hovered high over the counters. The counters themselves were heaped with bright, plentiful new stock for the Christmas season, and there would be music as soon as the doors opened for business.

They were rushing the season, it seemed to Cherry, but all the stores now followed this calendar of merchandising. She felt a little relieved, all the same, to step out of the elevator on the sixth floor and find that it was still November here, without any trace of decorations.

Of course there was decoration and beauty enough in the glass cases and fine furniture of the antiques department, where the night watchman was making the last of his rounds. The big personnel department, at the far end of this floor, was already bustling with activity, hiring new employees for the seasonal rush.

"Good morning, Miss Ames, good morning," her assistant sang out as Cherry entered the medical department. "How are we this morning?"

"Oh, just fine, I guess, Gladys. How are you?"

Gladys Green was a brand-new, young R.N., bouncing with enthusiasm. This was her first job and Cherry wished Gladys were a shade less determined to do good. She had, Cherry saw, rearranged the first-aid cabinet, the nursing instruments, and even, in the small partitioned room beyond, moved the two cots.

"Better, isn't it?" Gladys said cheerfully.

"It's very nice, though you'll have to show me where you've put things."

The infirmary, like most store infirmaries, was small and compact enough for her to be able to find things. Only small emergencies were treated here; anyone seriously ill would be treated by Dr. Murphy, whose office was around the corner. Absences due to illness were checked by the personnel department working together with the State Bureau of Compensation. Nursing here, Cherry reflected as she changed into white uniform and cap and white shoes, did not call on the more difficult nursing skills, like surgery or obstetrics, but it did place her on her own in full charge. Sound judgment about people and rapid, right decisions about health were the main requirements.

Gladys Green rose respectfully, to permit Cherry to occupy the one desk.

"Thanks, Gladys. Did you have any emergencies during the few days I was away?"

"Honestly, it was so quiet I didn't know what to do with myself! To tell you the truth, that's *half* the reason why I moved the equipment around."

Cherry grinned. "May I see the daily report sheets?"

Gladys gave them to her, then stood reading them solemnly over Cherry's shoulder.

"You did very well," Cherry said, reading: a cut finger; a sprained ankle; a head cold; a few other small emergencies. Then there was a woman customer who fell on the escalator, and a man in the shipping room who received a deep cut from broken glass. Nurse Green had administered first aid and sent them, with a store escort, to Dr. Murphy.

"I'll bet you I could have treated them perfectly well myself," the young nurse said.

"I'll bet you couldn't. I'll bet *I* couldn't. Any nurse who tries to play doctor isn't a very responsible nurse, you know."

"That's just what Ann Powell told me."

"Cheer up, Gladys, we won't have many slow periods now that Christmas shopping is starting."

"You're right. Listen." The hum of many people walking and talking, the metallic click of elevator doors, telephones ringing, indicated that the store was open now to customers.

This was a good chance, Cherry said, for them to check on supplies, and put the medical department in shipshape order. And Cherry took care to praise her assistant, who was trying so hard to do a good job.

The two nurses had been working for about an hour when someone knocked on the open door. It was Tom Reese, holding by the hand a small, tear-smudged boy.

"Good morning, Miss Ames. How would you like to take care of a young fellow who got separated from his mother?"

Cherry smiled at Tom Reese who looked startingly like her, vividly dark, lively, quick-moving—like more of a twin than Charlie. Then Cherry smiled at the youngster and held out her hand.

"I was just wishing for a boy to help me count boxes. What's your name?"

"Bobby. I want my mamma."

"Your mamma will be here in a few minutes. How high can you count, Bobby?"

The small boy stopped to think. "Twenty-five. Have you got more'n twenty-five boxes?"

"Well, we'd better go see. First, Miss Green, let's help Bobby off with his heavy coat, and give him a drink of water."

Gladys took charge of Bobby for the moment, and Cherry turned to Tom Reese. He explained that the child's mother would quickly be located via the store's loudspeaker system. Then he said:

"I can count to a million or so, if you'll need another helper. Did you have a good trip home?"

"Awfully good, thank you."

Tom Reese's dark eyes sparkled with friendliness. "Brace yourself for the big rush. If you need me, remember my office is right next door."

As he left, Gladys looked up from washing Bobby's face, a knowing grin on her face. Cherry pretended to pay no attention, and Bobby declared,

"That man's nice!"

Bobby's mother arrived soon afterward, and then a small stream of minor casualties kept Cherry and her assistant occupied. A man from the upholstery department came in holding a handkerchief over one eye. Cherry carefully, deftly, removed the lint particle which could cause surprising pain. Then she applied a soothing hot compress. "Don't rub your eyes," she cautioned the patient, "and don't use eye cups. Their pressure is harmful, and they can carry infection. If your eye feels sensitive, come back and I'll bathe it with a weak boric acid solution—using a sterilized eye dropper." The man thanked her and said he'd learned something.

A brief lull was interrupted by a saleswoman who complained of a sore throat. Cherry checked the woman over and said, "That 'sore throat' looks to me like strep throat, Mrs. Crane." Strep was infectious and everyone in this woman's department might catch it. "I'd like you to visit Dr. Murphy at once, Mrs. Crane. I'll phone him, and Miss Green will make out a medical pass for you to give your supervisor—"

So it went, all day Friday. Nothing crucial, but every case was important.

The next day there was no free time. Cherry and Gladys Green treated an assortment of customers and employees for minor ailments. Tom Reese poked his head in the door around noon to say:

"The main floor is beginning to look like a football scrimmage. Busy in here?"

"Well, I'd say we're earning our salaries," Cherry smiled back at him. "But I'm glad to be on a comparatively quiet floor. Antiques, apparently, are too costly to attract crowds."

"You should see the toy department. That reminds me! I'll have some toys sent here, because you two gals are going to have *lots* more mislaid children."

"Thank you, Mr. Reese."

"Everybody calls me Tom." He waved and was gone.

By Saturday evening Cherry was glad enough to go home to No. 9 and just sit down in the one comfortable armchair.

Only Bertha and Gwen were there, the others having gone out to a favorite restaurant around the corner. Bertha, who was No. 9's best and therefore chief cook, seemed rather hurt.

"Never mind," said Cherry to the big, handsome girl who still retained the wholesome outdoor look of a farm girl. "The three of us will rustle up something better than they can buy."

Gwen kicked off her shoes and flopped down on the sofa. "Jeepers, what a day! I like lab work, all except the standing up part. No, you *know* I can't work properly perched on a stool. Dr. Hall still doesn't believe that!"

They chatted a bit about their respective jobs. Bertha was in charge of a children's hospital ward and loved it. Privately they agreed they would not enjoy Betty Lane's job as nurse companion to a well-to-do elderly woman. They'd rather do real nursing. Somehow talking together quickened their professional pride and erased the day's trivial annoyances. Cherry turned on the radio for music, and Gwen, with a grandiloquent air, passed a tray of tomato-juice cocktails. Presently Bertha rustled up supper. They were having such a comfortable time as a threesome that it startled them when the telephone rang.

Gwen's aunt was calling from Long Island, with an interesting offer. Gwen relayed it to Cherry and Bertha.... "Yes, I'm listening to you, Aunt Kathy.... Hey, kids, she wants me and one of you Spencer Clubbers to stay with her for a while!"

"Where?" Cherry murmured. She felt an interest, since she and Gwen were old tried-and-true roommates.

"Long Island.... Where is Uncle John going on Sunday? ... Arabia? Good heavens!"

Bertha muttered something about Gwen's uncle being in the oil business. Gwen's face changed expression so rapidly that the other two could not figure out the rest of the conversation. Gwen hung up.

"Aunt Kathy is a love. She says she wants young company in that big house, and whichever two of us—"

A scrambling at the door interrupted them. The door suddenly swung open and Vivian, Mai Lee, and Betty Lane all but fell in. "I told you someone would forget to lock it again!" Vivian insisted, picking up her hat from the floor. Cherry had to smile at the sight of them. Mai Lee was tiny, like an ivory figurine; Vivian was a pretty girl of middle height; while Betty Lane rose to six feet, managing to look stately and dignified—which she wasn't.

"Good morning, welcome home, and good evening, Cherry," said Mai Lee and composedly sat down.

Betty Lane inquired if everybody's Thanksgiving had been as happy as hers.

"Terrific, except that's ancient history by now." Gwen moved over and made room on the sofa. The young women commenced to chatter.

"Has anyone seen Ann Evans this week? Are she and her husband back from Boston yet?"

"Who's the stunning young man who drives you home from work, Betty? You never told us you have a beau."

"Whoever took my thermometer by mistake," Vivian said plaintively, "please give it back by tomorrow. Somebody here has two."

Gwen raised her voice to announce that her aunt had room for an extra, unspecified Spencer Clubber and in the interests of democratic procedure she, Gwen, was giving one and all present a chance to accept. No one heard her, except Cherry.

"Shall I make my announcement all over again?"

"No, please don't—because I'd like to live out on Long Island with you," Cherry said. "I love being cramped in No. 9, but—"

"I was hoping for that." Gwen's crinkled-up eyes seemed to dance. "Commuting, I warn you. Though you're welcome to use my car out there. Now, how soon can you get a day off to move out there?"

"I'll find out. What day is good for you?"

Gwen and Cherry compared dates. Bertha and Betty argued about the merits of a new prosthetic device, while Mai Lee and Vivian shared the telephone in a visit with Ann.

"The Spencer Club," said Cherry to Gwen, "won't realize two of its tenants are going until we've actually gone. Try again to tell them, why don't you? And you know—I'm just delighted."

After a good rest on Sunday, Cherry reported for work bright and early Monday morning. Her eager